D0399849

Sable Hamilton

STARDUST STABLES

Free Spirit

STONE ARCH BOOKS
a capstone imprint

Stardust Stables is published by Stone Arch Books
A Capstone Imprint
1710 Roe Crest Drive
North Mankato, Minnesota 56003
www.capstoneyoungreaders.com

First published by
Stripes Publishing Ltd
1 The Coda Centre, 189 Munster Road
London SW6 6AW
Text © Jenny Oldfield, 2014
Cover © Stripes Publishing Ltd, 2014
Photographic images courtesy of www.istockphoto.com
© Pamela Moor and www.shutterstock.com

All Rights Reserved.

No part of this publication may be reproduced in whole or in part,
or stored in a retrieval system, or transmitted in any form or by any
means, electronic, mechanical, photocopying, recording, or otherwise,
without written permission of the publisher.

Library of Congress Cataloging-in-Publication Data is available
on the Library of Congress website.

ISBN: 978-1-4342-9792-1 (library binding)
ISBN: 978-1-4342-9796-9 (paperback)
ISBN: 978-1-4965-0208-7 (eBook PDF)

Summary: Kellie is in the remote mountains of Colorado filming a
movie. When disaster strikes, will she be the one to save the day?

Designer: Alison Thiele

Artistic Elements: Shutterstock

Printed in China.
092014   008472RRDS15

For Shelley, my fearless friend

Chapter 1

"Dylan was amazing!" Kellie said.

She sat with Alisa, Hayley, and Kami under the yellow umbrella outside the tack room at Stardust Stables. "You should've seen him on set, with the cameras rolling, pushing a dozen or more cows and calves across a river, and doing it single-handed. It was honestly out of this world!"

"Yeah, he's a great cow horse," Alisa agreed.

Kellie and Dylan had just flown in from Texas where they'd been working on a major movie called *Silver Spur*. Now they were back at Stardust in the mountains of Colorado, planning to take a well-earned break.

"I'm guessing so was his rider — out of this world," Kami reminded Kellie. In the few short weeks since she'd joined the junior stunt-riding team at Stardust, she'd met lots of talented riders, but none with Kellie's sheer, gutsy determination.

Kellie grinned and took a swig from her can of Coke. "I'd be nothing without him," she said modestly.

"That's true of all of us." Hayley didn't beat around the bush. She and Cool Kid, Alisa and Diabolo, Kami and Magic, Kellie and Dylan — great stunt riding relied on perfect teamwork between horse and rider.

"So what jobs are next?" Kellie wondered, loosening her wavy brown hair from its braid. She looked out across the empty corral toward the meadow where the horses grazed in the evening sun.

"There aren't any," said Alisa. Earlier that day, she had overheard stable-owner Lizzie Jones talking on the phone to various contacts in the movie business. "Lizzie's working really hard to get new contracts, but right now there's nothing happening."

Hayley sighed at the gloomy news, especially since she was the only girl rider who hadn't managed to secure a contract so far this summer, but Kellie refused to be downhearted.

"Hey," she said. "You can bet your life that the next job is just around the corner. Meanwhile, look at what we've got, right in front of our noses." She spread her hands and invited the other girls to take in the view.

"Beautiful sky and mountains," Hayley agreed.

"A bunch of great buddies," Kami said. Her new friends meant the world to her, and she wanted to make sure they knew it.

"Fantastic horses," Alisa added.

"Yeah, the horses," said Kellie with a sigh, gazing at Dylan taking a drink from the cool, clear creek. "When you think about it, life really doesn't get much better!"

∽ ⊛ ∾

"Don't you just thank your lucky stars?" Kellie asked Dylan.

Stars were on her mind. She had gotten out of bed at midnight, unable to sleep, put on her jeans, T-shirt, and boots, then walked out to the quiet meadow. A million stars twinkled, and a crescent moon shone. Spotting her approach, Dylan had come up to where she perched on the fence. He pushed his nose against her shoulder, nudging her so hard that she almost fell backward onto the dirt track that went around the meadow.

"Hey, quit that!" she said with a laugh. "Here I am talking about how lucky we are to be doing what we're doing, and you're not even listening!"

Dylan nuzzled up more gently this time.

"That's better. I mean — look at the stars. See the Milky Way? And Orion? And that mountain over there — that's Clearwater Peak. No, not that way — this way!" She looped her arm around Dylan's neck and turned his head in the right direction. "The one that's shaped like a giant Egyptian pyramid."

It was a view she'd known all her life. At 14,000 feet, Clearwater Peak was visible from the home in Colorado Springs she shared with her mom and dad and her fellow-stunt-rider brother, Tom. She knew all the hiking trails through the Clearwater National Forest, the picnic spots, and the camping grounds. Best of all, though, were the white-water rapids racing between granite boulders, alternating with stretches of the cold, clear, winding water of the South Platte River.

"This is going to sound stupid," she murmured, her arm still looped around Dylan's neck. "But you know how this night sky makes me feel?"

He stood perfectly still, ears pricked, gazing toward the distant peaks.

"I look up at the stars and I feel small," she whispered. "We're just tiny specks, you and me." Dylan turned his beautiful head toward her, his eyes like dark pools. "But that's okay," she continued. "It means two things — one, we're almost invisible, and two, we're totally free!"

∽ ◦ ℮

The next day, Saturday, was a lazy day at Stardust Stables.

"Hey, guys — Lizzie and Jack gave us all the morning off!" Tom announced at breakfast with his usual mischievous grin.

"Except for cleaning tack, hosing down saddle blankets, and taking alfalfa out to the meadow," Zak added with a grimace.

"Cool — no scooping poop." This was what pleased Ross the most. Leaving the horses out in the meadow meant that the corral would stay poop-free all day long. Like all the riders at Stardust, Ross loved the training and the camaraderie, but the chores? Not so much.

Only Kellie was unhappy — there were new stunts she wanted to try out with Dylan. That was until Becca showed up with an idea.

"What do you say we saddle up and take the horses along the Jeep trail?" Becca suggested to the girls. "I want to try cross-country loping through the pines trees along the ridge."

Kellie gave up on the idea of learning new stunts and headed straight out to the meadow. After all, what could be better than a relaxed, girls-only ride?

"Great — count me in!" Alisa cried. Then before they knew it, Hayley and Kami were also coming.

By eight o'clock, five girls and their horses were ready to set out from the corral, complete with bagged lunches and bottles of water.

"Formation trotting?" Hayley suggested as they eased out onto the dirt track. She and Cool Kid headed the group, with Alisa and Diabolo and Kellie and Dylan close behind, then Kami and Magic. Becca and Pepper brought up the rear.

"Ta-ra-ta-raah!" From the meadow, Zak cupped his hand to his mouth and imitated the sound of a cavalry trumpet. "Hey, girls — enjoy!" he yelled after them.

"We will!" Kellie called over her shoulder.

They took it gently until they hit the steep

Jeep trail heading toward the pine trees. Then, still in tight formation, they broke into a trot.

"Link hands?" Alisa suggested to Kellie. It meant that Diabolo and Dylan had to keep pace exactly, which was tricky since Diabolo had longer legs and a wider stride than Dylan. Soon, though, the two girls had their horses working in perfect unison.

"Ready to do some cross-country loping?" Hayley asked as they came up the hill.

At her signal, all five horses and riders left the trail and spread out among the trees. Kellie grinned as Dylan transitioned into a lope and then into a full gallop. Covering the soft ground at top speed, she swerved around a boulder then immediately ducked to avoid a low branch. She spotted a fallen tree ahead and adjusted her balance to allow Dylan to fly over it without a second thought.

"Good boy!" she breathed as he landed and galloped on. Freedom! This was exactly what she'd meant when she and Dylan had shared that moment under the stars.

By 1:30 p.m. the girls were heading back to the stables. They'd spent the morning loping through the forest and then picnicked in a high meadow. There they ate peanut butter and jelly sandwiches and watched tiny squirrels scamper to pick up the breadcrumbs before disappearing with a quick whisk of their bushy tails.

They remounted their horses and ambled back down the Jeep road until they came within sight of Elk Creek and the Stardust barn.

"Hey, Dylan, what's up?" Kellie asked when he suddenly ducked his head and skittered sideways.

Pepper, Magic, and Diabolo also started acting as if something had spooked them. Becca, Kami, and Alisa tightened their reins to hold them back. The girls didn't have long to wait before they found out what was wrong.

"Stick 'em up!" Without warning, Zak, Tom, and Ross jumped out from behind a big boulder. They pulled tough-guy faces and pointed pretend guns at the girls. But the guns were harmless twigs and the boys quickly dropped the charade and hooted with laughter.

"Gotcha!" they cried.

"Not funny!" Kellie cried. Dylan stopped

suddenly and threw her forward in the saddle, then crow-hopped off the path into some thorn bushes. "Jeez, thanks, guys!" she exclaimed sarcastically as she struggled to regain her balance.

Meanwhile, Cool Kid carried Hayley sideways into a group of spiky yucca plants. "Yeah, what was that about?" she demanded.

The boys stopped laughing and waited for the girls to regain control of their horses.

Embarrassed, Tom tried to explain. "We decided to hike up the Jeep trail, that's all. Ambushing you was a spur-of-the-moment thing."

"And it scared our horses half to death," Alisa pointed out.

"Sorry — it was my idea," Tom admitted. "I guess it was pretty childish."

"Totally," Kellie grumbled. Dylan's tail was tangled in a thorn bush and he had to struggle to free himself. Soon, though, all five girls were safely back on the trail.

Tom cleared his throat and gave Kami a sheepish smile. "Are you okay?" he asked, worried that his thoughtless prank would come between them.

"Fine, thanks," she said coolly.

"See you at dinner," he mumbled as he and the other two boys stood to one side. "I'll save you a seat."

"Don't hold your breath," Kellie warned her brother as she led the way downhill. *Serves him right*, she decided. Maybe next time the boys would think twice before pulling a stupid trick like that.

∽ ◦ ᧐

"Sorry," Tom told Kami at dinner that night. "We just didn't think."

"It's okay. Nothing bad happened." She sat down next to him, opposite Kellie and Hayley. As far as she was concerned, the boys' lunchtime prank was forgotten.

"Anyway, we've heard some good news." Eager to change the subject, Tom rushed to share the information he'd picked up from Jack, Lizzie's partner and co-boss of Stardust Stables. "Have you heard of a movie director named Jeb Burns?"

"Nope," Kellie said. "Should we have?"

"Probably not. He's not a big name — not yet,

anyway. But listen to this — he called Jack earlier today and told him about a movie he wants to shoot called *Welcome the Wind*."

The girls sat with forks poised over their pasta supper. "And?" Hayley urged.

"Jeb Burns went to film school with Jack so they go way back. *Welcome the Wind* is his pet project. It's about a family of poor sharecroppers in the 1930s."

"What's a sharecropper?" Kellie wanted to know.

"A farm worker who moved around the country looking for work," Tom answered. Relieved that Kellie wanted to talk to him again, Tom went on with his explanation. "Anyway, according to Jack, Jeb has finally managed to get the money together to start filming."

"And?" Hayley prompted.

"And he wants to hire a stunt rider from Stardust."

"Male or female?" asked Kellie.

"A girl."

"That's great news!" Kami said. "When's this Jeb guy planning to hold the audition?"

"Wednesday," Tom reported. "So hold on to your hat. Exciting things are about to happen."

Chapter 2

In the girls' dorm that night, all they talked about was *Welcome the Wind*. "I wonder who'll get chosen," Kami said wistfully as they sat with their feet up in the living area. She hoped it would be her and Magic, but she knew she'd have stiff competition in Becca, Alisa, Hayley, and Kellie.

"At least we know it's going to be someone from here," Hayley pointed out, hoping that this might be her big chance to finally get that contract.

"Do we?" Becca asked.

Kellie nodded. "According to Tom, High Noon isn't in the picture this time."

High Noon Stables was run by Pete Mason, Lizzie's ex-husband, and the competition between the two outfits was often intense. To make things worse, Mason was a mean and dishonest rival.

"Thank goodness," Alisa sighed. At least it would be a clean contest between the Stardust riders and the best person would be chosen.

"So, girls, you'd better watch out!" Hayley declared, jumping up with a grin on her face. "Cool Kid and me, we'll be going all out!"

"Good night, we love you too!" Kellie called after her as Hayley scooted off to the bedroom they shared.

Alisa stood up and raked through the embers dying in the grate before closing the door of the wood-burning stove. "Time for some shut-eye," she yawned.

"Same here," said Kami, and the two girls disappeared off to bed with a wave.

"So who will it be?" Kellie asked Becca when they were the only ones left in the room.

Becca shrugged. "Whoever looks right, I guess."

Kellie nodded. She knew it was important for an actor and stunt rider to look similar, but there would be more to it than that. "Yeah, and whoever rides best," she added. "So watch out, Bex — Dylan and I are gonna kick butt!"

∽ ◦ ⌒

"I can't wait for Wednesday!" Hayley was the first one up next morning and the first out in the meadow to fetch Cool Kid from the corral. She was brushing dirt out of her Paint's brown and white coat when Kellie showed up.

"Me neither," Kellie murmured as she took a halter and lead rope from the hook in the tack room. "I guess all the girls here have a chance at the part," she said with a grin. "With that in mind, I need to put in a little extra work on my vaulting technique."

"Me too," Hayley told her.

"Why don't you go ahead into the round pen while I fetch Dylan?" Slinging the halter and rope over her shoulder, Kellie made her way along the side of the old, red-roofed barn toward the meadow. She whistled as she walked, enjoying the freshness of the morning.

In her mind, she went through the vaulting routine she and Dylan would rehearse. She would set him off at a lope for a full circuit of the round pen, standing in the middle and watching him pick up speed — once, twice around the pen, counting out the number of steps she would need to take. Then she would run until she came alongside him, place both hands on his rump, and like a gymnast she would vault onto his back. Dylan wouldn't miss a beat. He would lope on evenly while she dismounted then vaulted again — maybe five or six times until the trick had been perfected. She hoped the routine would impress Jeb Burns at the audition in three days.

Kellie was still whistling when she came to the meadow and opened the gate. She smiled as Kami's dappled gray horse, Magic, trotted up and nuzzled at her pocket for a treat that wasn't there. "Sorry, not today," she told him, looking around for Dylan. She spotted him down by the creek.

That's weird, she thought. Normally her boy would raise his head at her approach and come trotting to meet her. But today he stood and watched uneasily from the water's edge. She walked toward him. "Hey, Dylan — are you ready to get to work?"

Dylan stayed put. "What's up?" she asked, unslinging the rope from her shoulder.

He whinnied softly, but he still didn't move.

A small knot formed in her stomach. "No, really — is something wrong?"

He swished his tail and took a few uneven steps toward her.

"Oh no!" The moment he moved, Kellie saw what was the matter. Each time he put weight on his right front leg, he stumbled and then lifted the leg high off the ground. "You're hurting!" she cried.

She ran to him and dropped to her knees, running the palm of her hand up and down his leg until she felt it — a painful, hot swelling in the joint. "How?" she exclaimed. "What happened? Did one of the other horses kick you?"

Dylan gave her a sorrowful look.

"Don't worry," she murmured. "You're going to be just fine, I promise."

∽ ◦ ᴄ∽

"Hey, Kellie, what's up?" Ross asked as she led Dylan into the barn.

Dylan was the picture of dejection as he limped along.

"What's it look like? He's hurt," Kellie snapped. The knot in her stomach had tightened. Although she'd tried to sound cheerful for Dylan's sake, she was feeling awful.

Zak and Tom put down their rakes and joined Ross at the barn door.

"You want me to tell Lizzie?" Zak offered.

"Yeah, she should know," Tom added.

"Not yet. Let me take a look first." Guiding Dylan into one of the wooden stalls, Kellie stooped to examine the swollen joint. "I'm thinking maybe he got kicked by one of the other horses out in the meadow," she muttered. In which case, the leg would be bruised, but hopefully the swelling would go down soon.

"Let's hope he's okay by Wednesday," said Ross. He voiced what everyone was thinking.

"Easy, boy!" Kellie said as she ran her fingertips over the swelling and Dylan winced. "Oh, jeez!" she groaned as she felt a crust of dried blood and a small, hard point — something lodged beneath the skin. Dylan edged backward and gave a short whinny.

"He didn't get kicked," Kellie said slowly. "This happened yesterday when we were out on the Jeep trail."

"Why? What is it?" Tom came into the stall, standing in a shaft of sunlight. He raised a hand to shield his eyes.

"It's a thorn," Kellie told him angrily. "From when you jumped out from behind that rock and sent Dylan crashing into the bush."

"Let me see," Tom offered.

But Kellie blocked his way. "Haven't you done enough already?" she said. "Dylan picked up a thorn from the bush — it's gone deep into the joint and now it's probably infected."

"Look, I'm sorry. I didn't mean . . ."

"Do you realize what you've done?" Kellie yelled at her brother, tears stinging her eyes.

"I said I'm sorry."

Quickly, Ross stepped in. "Back off, Tom," he advised. "Don't you see what she's saying? If Dylan's leg doesn't heal before Wednesday, you've wrecked their chances of auditioning for *Welcome the Wind*."

∽ ◦ ℰ

Zak ran to the ranch house to get Lizzie, in spite of what Kellie had said.

"Kellie's mad at us," he explained as the owner of Stardust Stables hurried to the barn. "It's our fault because we spooked Dylan and he ended up in a thorn bush."

"When was that?"

"Yesterday, out on the Jeep trail. We jumped out from behind a rock."

Lizzie shook her head. "I'm disappointed. Don't you boys know better than to pull a trick like that?"

∽ ◦ ℃

By the time she reached Dylan's stall, Lizzie had gotten all the information she needed from Zak. She asked the three boys to leave the stall clear for her and Kellie to treat the puncture wound in Dylan's leg.

"Here's what we do," she said calmly. "First we wash out the wound with saline solution. That's two teaspoons of salt to four cups of boiled water. You think you can make that for us?" she asked Zak, who nodded.

"You can actually feel the end of the thorn," Kellie told her, relieved that Lizzie was there after all. "It's a hard spike. I tried to take it out, but he won't stand still long enough to let me get it — I guess it hurts too much."

"That's okay. We will have to clean the area around the wound first, open it up, and then use a pair of tweezers to take out the thorn." Expertly feeling the swollen joint while Kellie held Dylan steady, Lizzie's expression was serious. "The bad thing is that we didn't notice this right away, which means that some bacteria has started to get to work and cause an infection. Plus, a puncture wound like this may look small and harmless, but it can go deep into the joint and affect the underlying structures."

Kellie stayed close to Dylan and tried to soothe him. "It's going to be okay," she whispered as she stroked his mane. Dylan listened to Kellie's calming words and stood patiently. Zak came back with the saline solution and a first-aid kit before quietly slipping away.

"All right. Here we go." Lizzie rolled back the sleeves of her plaid shirt and put on a pair of blue latex gloves. She dipped a gauze pad into the rapidly cooling solution and then pressed it onto the wound.

"Easy!" Kellie whispered in Dylan's ear.

"Luckily Dylan is up to date with all his tetanus shots, so we don't have to worry about that," Lizzie reassured Kellie as she worked. "And there's no nasty discharge from the wound, so hopefully this should heal nice and quickly once we've removed the thorn."

"You have to be a brave boy," Kellie urged Dylan as Lizzie took some tweezers out of a sterile packet. With a steady hand, she peeled back the broken skin and eased the steel points into position. "Hold really still — it'll all be over soon."

Dylan turned his head toward her and didn't flinch as Lizzie carefully pulled out an inch-long thorn.

"It came out in one piece — perfect!" Lizzie held up the thorn for inspection. She asked Kellie to pass her a tube of antibacterial ointment and a bandage from the first-aid kit. She smoothed the ointment onto the wound, then methodically began wrapping Dylan's leg. "Hopefully the cream will clear up the infection and the bandage will minimize movement in the leg until the swelling goes down."

"Will he need box-rest?" Kellie wanted to know.

Lizzie nodded. "For a couple of days while we change the dressings."

"You hear that? No running around in the meadow until this heals," Kellie told Dylan. Then she came out with the question that had been lurking at the back of her mind all along. "What do you think — will he be okay for the *Welcome the Wind* audition?"

Lizzie took off her gloves and closed up the first-aid kit. With her head to one side, she studied Kellie and Dylan closely. "Never say never," she said quietly. "I honestly don't know, but we've done all we can. Now we'll just have to wait and see."

Chapter 3

"Dylan hates being cooped up — it drives him crazy," Kellie said with a sigh.

It was Monday morning, just after dawn. She and Kami were the only two people awake and already at work in the barn. Kellie tipped grain pellets into Dylan's feeder while Kami mucked out his stall.

"But he kept his bandage on," Kami pointed out. "He didn't try to chew it off."

"Yeah, you're a good patient!" Kellie told her horse, trying to hide her worry as she began to brush dust and straw from his dark coat and mane.

"Have you talked to Tom yet?" Kami asked quietly.

Kellie shook her head. "I've got nothing to say to him."

"I spoke with him late last night," said Kami,

heaping muck into a wheelbarrow. "He's really sorry, you know."

Kellie still wasn't in the mood to forgive. "He can be sorry all he wants. It doesn't change the fact that Dylan got hurt."

Kami nodded uncomfortably. She hated that Tom and Kellie weren't speaking since she was close to both of them.

Kellie glanced at her. "Sorry if you feel like you're stuck between me and Tom," she said. "But my brother's been an idiot."

"Along with Zak and Ross," Kami gently reminded her.

"Yeah, but it was all Tom's idea." Kellie brushed Dylan's coat until it gleamed in the early morning sun.

"Are you more angry with him or scared for Dylan?" Kami wondered.

Kellie looked up again and rested the brush against Dylan's neck. "Both." She sighed. "But honestly, Kami, I just want Dylan to be well again. That's all I care about right now."

∽ ◉ ℃

"Breakfast by the creek!" Jack announced as

Alisa, Becca, and Hayley emerged sleepily from the girls' dorm. "Get a move on, girls — we have a visitor."

"What's going on with Jack?" Hayley asked, nudging Alisa. "Why's he in such a good mood so early in the day?"

"What do you mean? He's always happy," Alisa countered as they headed for the lawn where bacon was being fried over an open fire. As usual, she was the only one without a serious case of bed-head and crumpled-shirt.

"Yeah, but he's wearing his best boots and Stetson. Plus he's got a big grin on his face."

As soon as the girls reached the cookout, they realized that Hayley was right — something special was happening.

"Alisa, Hayley — meet Jeb Burns," Lizzie said. "He was in the area on business so he decided to drop by. Ross went to round up the others. Why don't you two sit and chat with him?"

It turned out that Jack's director-buddy had movie-star looks. He was tall and lean, with clear gray eyes set in a tanned, square-jawed face. *He should've been in front of the camera, not behind it,* Alisa decided.

"Time to make a good impression," Hayley

whispered to Alisa. She stepped forward to shake the director's hand. "So, Jeb, we'd like to know more about your movie," she began.

"What can I tell you?" Jeb took a plate of bacon and eggs from Lizzie, who offered him blueberry pancakes as well. "No pancakes, thanks. I'm watching my waistline." He went with Alisa and Hayley to sit at a table overlooking the creek. "We hope to shoot it here in Colorado or maybe Wyoming. My location manager and I are still looking for the perfect setting.

"My family lives in Wyoming," Hayley said enthusiastically. "At the foot of the Teton Mountains, outside of Jackson Hole. It'd make a great location."

Jeb made a mental note. "Thanks. I've signed up a lead actress called Jemma Scott — she's totally unknown, straight out of high school. This is her first acting role."

"You'll probably meet her on Wednesday," Jack interrupted as he came around with the coffee. "That right, Jeb?"

The director nodded. "Yeah, I'd like her to meet you guys, see how she acts around horses and give her a chance to meet the rider who's going to be her stunt double."

"Cool," Alisa said with a flutter of excitement. Then she noticed Jeb suddenly sit up and pay attention to something happening behind them. When she glanced over her shoulder she saw that Kellie and Kami were hurrying to join them at the cookout.

"Who's that?" Jeb asked.

"The girl with the blond hair is my roommate, Kami," Alisa told him.

"No, the other one — the one with the crazy curls."

"That's Kellie," Hayley cut in.

"Amazing." Jeb shook his head in disbelief. "The hair, the way she walks — everything!"

"What?" asked the girls in unison.

"She looks exactly the same as Jemma," he replied. "I swear, they're two peas in a pod!"

∽ ◦ ⌒

"So what did you think?" Kami asked Kellie. Jeb Burns had finished his breakfast and driven to Denver to meet up with his scriptwriters and location manager. The two girls had gone back to work in the barn.

"He's cool," Kellie replied. "I like him."

"And he liked you." Kami recalled how the director had separated Kellie off from the other young riders and told her about his plans for the movie. "It was totally obvious," she added with a touch of envy.

"He said that one of the major stunts involves working with a vintage truck." Kellie frowned. "Dylan likes cows. I'm not sure that he'd be any good around smelly, noisy vehicles. And that's even if he gets to audition — which he might not because — you know . . ."

Aware that her horse could overhear their conversation from his stall, Kellie stopped talking.

Kami's face broke into a grin. "You know he's a horse, right? He can't actually understand what we're saying."

"Don't be too sure," Kellie argued. She was growing used to the fact that Dylan might miss Wednesday's audition, so she decided to play down their chances. "Anyway, I'm not holding my breath."

Kami chucked the last bale onto the trailer. She asked Kellie to help her hitch the trailer onto the tractor so they could drive out to the meadow. "Have you made friends with your brother yet?" she asked.

Kellie jumped up onto the tractor and switched on the engine. It lurched forward out of the barn. "Nope," she called back. "And I still don't want to talk about it. Are you coming or not?"

∽ ◦ ℘

The news about Dylan that afternoon wasn't great. "The joint is still swollen," Lizzie said, after she'd removed the bandage and examined the leg. "The antibiotic is doing its job because there's no discharge, but there's still the problem of inflammation."

Kellie sighed. "He's never going to be ready for the audition, is he?"

Lizzie frowned as she applied a new bandage. "It would be a pity if you didn't audition," she said quietly. "Jeb really seemed to like you."

"But he didn't know Dylan was injured," Kellie pointed out.

"No, but there's no rule that says you have to ride Dylan at the audition," Lizzie pointed out. "You could perform your stunts on one of the boys' horses."

The remark shot through Kellie like an arrow. "No way!" she cried. Dylan and Kellie, Kellie and Dylan — they were a team.

"Just listen. There's time for you to train with a different horse — actually a whole day — and this job means a lot to Stardust. It's the only one on our radar right now. Sometimes in this line of work, we have to be flexible. If Jeb comes back the day after tomorrow and still thinks you're the right girl for the job, he won't care whether you ride Dylan or Zak's Ziggy or Tom's Legend."

"No!" Kellie insisted. "That's not how it works."

Lizzie fastened the bandage and stood up with a sigh. "Think about it — okay?"

Kellie nodded reluctantly. She avoided saying anything else by leaving to fetch new straw for Dylan's bed.

"Just keep an open mind," Lizzie added, sliding carefully out of the stall before heading off to work with Becca, Alisa, Hayley, and Kami in the round pen.

∽ ◦ ∾

"So we park the truck across the gate," Lizzie instructed Zak while the girls and their horses waited in the corral. "We leave the brake on and the engine running. Each time a horse and rider tries to squeeze past you into the pen, you put your foot on the gas and make a lot of engine noise — okay?"

Eager to impress, Hayley and Cool Kid were the first to go. She felt her horse tense up as he got the smell of diesel in his nostrils. She had to press her legs against his sides to make him move forward. There was just enough room to squeeze between the gatepost and the noisy vehicle blocking the entrance. "Good boy," she murmured when he made it into the middle of the pen.

Becca came next on Pepper, then Alisa on Diabolo. Both had trouble convincing their horses to walk past the truck with its roaring engine and blinking red taillights. When it came to Kami's turn, Magic refused point blank to join them. He planted his feet, flared his nostrils, and laid his ears flat against his head.

"Never mind — I guess trucks just aren't his thing," Lizzie called. "We're not going to stress him out by putting too much pressure on him. You can unsaddle him and give him the day off."

If Kami was disappointed, she didn't let it show when she met Tom in the corral later. "It wasn't our day," she confessed. "Magic loves the ocean. He'll do any stunt you want if it involves water — rolling onto his back, swimming, loping through surf — anything. But it turns out he won't go near a truck."

"Every horse is different," Tom acknowledged. He stopped grooming Legend to help Kami loosen Magic's cinch, then offered to carry the saddle into the tack room while she led Magic out to the meadow. As he started heading into the tack room, he bumped into Kellie just as she emerged onto the porch carrying a halter.

"Whoa!" he cried before he had time to peer over the top of the saddle to see who was blocking his way.

"Sorry," she said, looking up. "Oh, it's you."

"Yeah, it's me, and now you're not sorry," he said as he slung Kami's saddle on to its rail. "In fact, I bet you wish you'd poked me in the eye with that buckle." He looked unhappy in spite of his jokey tone, and Kellie felt a pang of guilt. Then she thought of poor Dylan cooped up in the stall.

"Do you still hate me?" Tom asked.

"What do you think? We should be out there working in the round pen, Dylan and me."

"I know." There was a long, awkward silence.

"Hey, you didn't know it, but I was there in the barn earlier — when you and Lizzie were working on Dylan's leg. I heard what she said about you riding another horse for the audition."

"You had no right to snoop —" Kellie began.

Tom put up both hands in self-defense. "I was just there — I didn't do it on purpose! Anyway, I think Lizzie had a point."

Kellie shook her head. "You can't split Dylan and me. Just think — it would be like you riding Ziggy. It wouldn't work."

"You could try," he insisted, stepping out onto the porch with her. "Open mind, remember."

Kellie sighed. She stared at Tom's horse, Legend, alone in the corral. His honey-colored coat was spotless, and his blond mane and tail were shining like silk.

"Legend's great around motor vehicles," Tom reminded her quietly.

Kellie shot him a look then turned back to the Palomino.

"Why don't you just try?"

She took a deep breath and thought hard.

"Come on — you know you want to," Tom said with a slow, winning smile.

Chapter 4

"Give it a try," Alisa told Kellie. "Until Dylan gets better, why not try working with Legend?"

"I agree," Hayley said.

"Yeah, why not?" Kami and Becca chorused.

It was Monday evening and the girls were in the dorm, relaxing after a hard day's training. So far it had turned out that Hayley and Cool Kid were by far the best team for ignoring the roar of an engine and the smell of exhaust fumes. Alisa and Becca had needed to work hard to get Diabolo and Pepper to focus on their stunts, while Kami had reluctantly admitted that the job on *Welcome the Wind* was not for her and Magic.

"Tom would love for you to work with Legend. He told me so," Kami said. "He wants to make up for what they did."

"Which wasn't that bad when you think about it," Becca pointed out.

"He didn't mean for Dylan to get injured," Hayley reminded Kellie.

"Okay, okay!" Kellie grabbed her denim jacket and shoved her feet into her boots. "I'll think about it," she said. She slammed the door on her way out.

"Should we follow her?" Kami asked in the nervous silence that followed.

Alisa shook her head. "No, you know what Kellie's like — she needs her own space to work things out."

"Gotcha," Kami murmured, and she showed the others her crossed fingers.

"Don't worry, she'll get there in the end," Hayley added. "Just give her time."

∼⊙⊙

"It's not really Tom that I'm mad at." Kellie was in the barn with Dylan, sitting astride his stall door. Moonlight streamed in through the partition overlooking the meadow. "It's me. I blame myself for not keeping you safe."

Dylan came close and nuzzled her hand. "Okay, so neither of us knew you'd spook and get caught up in a thorn bush." Her horse nibbled the sleeve of her jacket and then rubbed his nose against her shoulder. "I just wish I'd seen the thorn in time. Now they want me to audition with Legend, and I'm saying, 'No — Dylan and I are a team. You can't separate us.'"

Dylan stopped rubbing and looked at her.

"It would be, you know . . . like I was letting you down."

He nudged her gently and let out a long sigh.

"But then again, you'd know I was only working with Legend until your leg was better. And at least it would give me the chance to show Jeb Burns what I can do."

Nudge, nudge, nibble. *Yes!* Dylan seemed to say.

"So you think it would be okay?" Kellie whispered.

Nudge and nuzzle. *Sure. Why not?*

"You really want me to do it?"

A strong nudge almost shoved Kellie off her perch. *Yeah, go for it!*

She regained her balance, and a wide grin spread across her face. The moon shone in and the stars twinkled. "Okay, I will!" she said.

∽ ◦ ⌣

The next morning, Jack intercepted Lizzie on the ranch-house porch and pointed out that Kellie and Legend had only twenty-four hours to learn how to work together. He'd seen her saddling Tom's horse in the corral and learned from a relieved Kami about Kellie's change of heart.

"I already know that. No need to rub it in."

"You think it's worth all the extra work?" he asked.

"I really do," Lizzie said. "And even if the audition doesn't go well tomorrow, it'll still be good experience for Kellie to ride a different horse."

"I guess you're right." Jack tilted back his hat and scratched his forehead. "Do we know how Legend is around vehicles?" he asked.

Lizzie shrugged. "Good, I think. Anyway, we're about to find out," she said, fixing her black Stetson firmly on her head.

It feels weird, was all Kellie could think as she tightened Legend's cinch and then stepped up into the saddle. Tom's Palomino was taller than Dylan, his neck longer, his head smaller and more refined. With his flowing blond mane and tail, he was a gorgeous horse.

"You two look really great," Tom told her. He had kept out of the way while she saddled Legend. But now that she was ready to ride him into the round pen, he stepped forward to wish her luck.

She nodded. "Thanks."

"So what's the plan?"

"Lizzie says to start with saddle falls and then move on to front wings."

"He'll do that, no problem," Tom told her. "Just watch to make sure he doesn't get too close to the outer rim during the falls. He could easily trap you against the fence rails, and I don't want to be scraping squished sister out of the dirt."

"Ha! Okay, thanks." She was about to ride off when she reined Legend back. "I mean it, Tom — thanks for letting me ride your horse."

"I wouldn't trust anyone except you," he told her. "Now, go get 'em!"

She grinned. "Watch me!" Then she urged Legend forward. Lizzie was waiting in the round pen. They had work to do.

∽ ◦ ⌒

"Let's do a basic saddle fall to the right," Lizzie

instructed as Kellie loped Legend clockwise around the pen.

Kellie had the trainer's attention, one on one, and she had to admit to herself that she felt a little nervous. Somehow Legend sensed the tension in his rider, as horses always do, so he swished his tail and flicked his ears.

Tom was right, Kellie realized — Legend did lope just a little too close to the fence, even though the truck sat in the entrance, its engine growling as they passed within a foot of where it stood. She decided to press with her left leg and neck rein him to the right. He understood and eased away from the fence. Better!

"On the count of three," Lizzie called over the sound of the engine. "One — two — three!"

Kellie kicked both feet free of the stirrups and flung herself toward the center of the pen. She hit the ground, rolled, and sprang to her feet unharmed.

"Not bad!" Lizzie told her. "We'll do two more to the right then three to the left, change direction to counterclockwise, and do it all over again. Then we'll take a break."

As Kellie caught up with Legend and vaulted back into the saddle, she noticed that three of the girls had gathered by the fence. Becca, Hayley, and Alisa were watching the stunts with interest.

"Let's take it a little faster this time," Kellie whispered to Legend, giving him a small kick as he switched into competition mode.

His lope became a full gallop.

"One — two — three!" Lizzie counted them down.

Kellie launched herself from the saddle, hit the ground, rolled, and sprang up.

"Wow, they're good!" Hayley said with a low whistle. "Legend pays no attention to the truck. It's as if it isn't even there."

"What do you reckon — will Jeb Burns be impressed?" Becca wondered.

"Yeah, he will. We'll definitely have to up our game if we want this job," Alisa predicted. "You watch — Kellie and Legend will be hard to beat!"

∾ ⊙ ℘

"Ouch!" Kellie's right shoulder was sore as she hoisted herself up to sit on the gate into Dylan's stall.

Time had flown by. It was already Tuesday evening, and her body was now paying the price for all the stunts that she'd been working on with Legend throughout the day.

"So I thought you'd want to know that it's going okay," she told Dylan. "It's not the same, obviously. I mean, there isn't the strong bond between me and Legend — not like the one between you and me. But we do a good enough job. In fact, I have to admit that Legend is one smart horse, besides looking spectacular, with that glossy mane and caramel coat."

Dylan edged toward her through the straw. A couple of hours earlier, Lizzie had decided to take off the heavy bandage binding his injured joint. Now he moved more easily, but his head was down and he seemed dejected.

"Don't look so sad," she murmured. "Lizzie says the swelling has finally gone down. She reckons you can go back into the meadow tomorrow morning — just for an hour or two to see how you do. Hey, you should be happy!"

He nudged her arm and nibbled her sleeve, as if to say, *"Remember me?"*

"Poor baby!" She jumped into the stall and wrapped both arms around his neck. "Don't be jealous," she whispered. "Sure, Legend's a good looker, but remember — looks are only skin deep.

He doesn't have your heart and your strength. I don't love him the same way I love you!"

∽ ◉ ℘

"Ready?" Alisa knocked on Kellie and Hayley's door at seven o'clock the next morning. It was Wednesday — a big day for Stardust. It was time for the girl stunt riders to impress.

"Uh-uh!" Hayley groaned. She came to the door in her faded stars-and-stripes pajamas. "What time is it?"

"Time to get ready and bring Cool Kid in from the meadow," Alisa reminded her. "Jeb Burns and Jemma Scott will be here in an hour. Where's Kellie?"

"Uh, dunno." Hayley grunted, then yawned.

"She's already out in the barn with Dylan," Kami reported from the door. "She said she was planning to lead him out into the meadow and then bring Legend back to the corral."

"You want me to bring Cool Kid for you?" Becca asked Hayley as she passed by. She was up and dressed in a crisp pale blue shirt and jeans, ready to fetch Pepper.

"Uh," Hayley said. "Puh-lease."

"See you out there," Alisa told her as she walked out into the bright morning sun.

∽ ◦ ⌣

The girls all had butterflies in their stomachs as a dusty blue Jeep drove into the yard. Even Kami, who was not auditioning, crossed her fingers as she watched Jeb Burns step down from the driver's seat.

The director went around to the passenger side to open the door for a slim girl with a mass of dark brown curls. She got out of the Jeep and waited to be introduced to Lizzie and Jack.

The girls watched carefully. If this was Jemma Scott, she lacked the look-at-me pizzazz that came with most of the young actresses they'd met.

"She looks . . . normal!" Hayley sounded so surprised that the others couldn't help smiling.

Jemma seemed shy as she shook hands with Lizzie. She was dressed in ordinary boot-cut jeans and a white shirt. It didn't look like she was wearing even a scrap of makeup.

"Forget 'normal'! More to the point, she looks exactly like you!" Alisa gasped. The resemblance was astonishing.

"Girls, come and meet the next big teen star!" Jack called across the yard. "It'll be cool — you'll be able to say you knew her before she was famous!"

The comment made Jemma blush as she said hello to the stunt riders.

"But she does — she looks totally normal," Hayley whispered to Kami, who was hanging back, not wanting to get in the way. "I bet she bought her shirt and jeans from a chain store."

"Hi." Becca was first in line to greet Jemma, followed by Alisa.

"My turn!" Hayley shot forward to introduce herself. "I'm Hayley. My horse is called Cool Kid. He's a brown and white Paint. Come and see — you're going to love him!"

"Kellie?" Lizzie prompted before Hayley had time to sweep Jemma away.

"Hi." Kellie blushed and stepped up to meet the young actress. A shy smile lingered around her wide mouth and her gray eyes sparkled as she hooked a strand of wavy hair behind her ear.

"Hi, Kellie," Jemma said, returning the smile.

"Wow!" Suddenly the resemblance struck Becca too. She couldn't stop the exclamation escaping from her lips.

"You two look — I mean — you two . . . !" It was no good — she was at a loss for words.

"Totally wow!" added Hayley.

The similarity between Kellie and Jemma was incredible — their hair, eyes, mannerisms, everything. They were practically identical. Definitely two peas in a pod, just like Jeb Burns had said.

Chapter 5

"So, you like horses?" Kami asked Jemma as they perched together on the round pen fence, waiting for the auditions to begin.

"Like them? I love them!" With the sun on her face and her dark hair gleaming, Jemma's natural beauty shone through. "When I was a little kid in Maryland, I wanted to have my own pony, but Mom could never scrape the money together. Instead I watched old cowboy movies on TV and hung around the local stable doing any job they'd give me."

"So you got to ride some?"

"Once in a while," Jemma nodded. "This movie role is heaven for me," she admitted. "I get to be around horses and get paid for it!"

"My guess is she'd pretty much act in the movie for free," Jeb commented as he and Jack joined the girls. "But we pay our actors union rates and do everything properly, including not letting Jemma do her own stunts and following the American Humane Association's rules," he explained. "Which means we only hire experienced stunt riders and well-trained horses."

"Speaking of, we're ready." Jack pointed to the gate where Alisa waited with Diabolo.

"Okay, you can go ahead," Jeb called.

Alisa took a deep breath and then entered the round pen at a lope. Her long, loose black hair was caught by the wind, and she looked cool and elegant in her pink shirt. Diabolo loped beautifully, knowing she was on show. She didn't alter her pace at all as Alisa went into spin-the-horn. Alisa then performed a vaulting dismount and sprinted across the middle of the arena to remount Diabolo, just as Becca and Pepper followed them into the pen.

"Jeez, they both look like they were born in the saddle!" Jemma murmured, her face alive with excitement. She gasped as Becca flung herself sideways and went into a front wing.

Becca hung on to the saddle horn with her left hand and leaned dangerously off balance toward Pepper's head, her right arm outstretched.

The onlookers shrank back from the grit kicked up by the horse's hooves as he sped by.

"Here comes Hayley!" Kami announced.

"Yee-hah!" Hayley took off her hat and waved it in the air, rodeo-style, as Cool Kid reared and pawed the air. He landed, rocked forward, and kicked out his hind legs. Hayley grinned, waved her hat again, and went on rearing, bucking, and yee-hahing around the arena.

"Wow!" Jemma breathed, while Jeb Burns asked Jack about Hayley's history as a stunt rider.

"Her mother is Gina Forest, the stunt-riding star of *Way Out West*, the eighties TV show. Gina put Hayley on horseback before she was three years old."

"Her mother passed on her talent for sure," Jeb commented. "Plus Hayley looks like she's having fun."

"Always," Jack agreed. He could tell the auditions were going well.

"But this is the kid I'm really interested in." Jeb's attention switched to Kellie and Legend — the final pair to enter the pen. "From where I'm standing, it looks like Lizzie has saved the best for last."

"Such a pretty horse!" Jemma exclaimed.

Kellie's mouth felt dry and her heart raced as she and Legend began. *Will yesterday's hard work pay off?* she wondered. She noticed Tom standing with Lizzie, Zak, and Ross on the tack-room porch. Her brother gave her a thumbs-up sign — *You can do it!*

Yes, we can! Kellie felt Legend ease into a smooth lope. He stuck close to the fence as always, neck stretched and ears flicked forward, tail and mane streaming in the wind. Kellie got ready for the vault tricks they'd rehearsed, waiting for Hayley, Alisa, and Becca to gather outside the pen.

Now there was space. As soon as she saw that the coast was clear, Kellie spun the horn and vaulted off, landed beautifully, then set off at a run after Legend. She vaulted back on then off again, totally focused on carrying out the stunts to the best of her ability. She forgot the bruises, aches, and pains of the training day and performed for Jeb Burns like the top-class athlete she was.

The director gave a single, brief nod. "Kellie's the one that I want," he told Jack. "To be honest with you, even before we began the auditions, there was never any doubt in my mind."

"Kellie it is!" Jack shook hands with Jeb. "Thanks, girls!" he called to Alisa, Hayley, and Becca. "You all did great, but Jeb has made his decision. The *Welcome the Wind* job goes to Kellie and Legend!"

∽ ◦ ℃

Kellie and Legend? Jack's words echoed in Kellie's ears as she rode Tom's horse from the round pen into the corral.

"Congratulations!" Hayley came up beside her on Cool Kid. She was heartbroken about not being chosen but determined not to show it.

"Yeah, really good job," Becca agreed. "Look at you, Kellie. You're hot property — straight from one contract to another."

"At least Jack and Lizzie can sleep a little easier," Alisa said. "Stardust really needs the income."

"Excellent!" Tom joined in the chorus of approval. He grabbed Legend's reins while Kellie slipped from the saddle. "Kami and I — we knew you could do it."

Kellie and Legend! Kellie couldn't get the unusual phrase out of her head. As she patted

Tom's horse and then took off his bridle, she thought how odd it sounded — how wrong. Still, she wanted to reward Legend for his hard work, so she headed to the barn for a handful of extra grain pellets.

She was sticking her hand into the grain barrel when Kami walked Dylan in from the meadow. "Lizzie said to bring him in for more box-rest," Kami explained.

"Yeah, okay." Hit by a sudden wave of guilt, Kellie couldn't think of anything else to say. Only when Dylan came up to her and nudged her hand for grain did she say hi to him. "How are you doing?" she murmured.

He tossed his head and nudged her hand until she opened it and let him snack.

"Did you hear what happened?" Kellie said quietly.

Dylan munched noisily on the grain.

"We . . . I . . . got the *Welcome the Wind* job." As she spoke, she became hot and shaky. She felt so guilty!

Her horse stopped eating and cocked his head sideways.

"The audition went well," Kellie told him. "Legend was great."

Dylan started to chew again — more slowly and thoughtfully this time.

Kellie nodded sadly. "Yeah, I know," she said with a sigh. "It just doesn't feel right."

∿ ◦ ᗡ

Jack and Lizzie invited Jeb and Jemma to stay for lunch.

"You guys are so lucky," Jemma told her new friends at Stardust. "You spend all day doing what you love."

"The same applies to you," Becca reminded her. "Most girls would kill to star in a movie."

"Anyway, we only work at Stardust during the summer," Hayley pointed out, her mouth full of salad. "The rest of the year we go home and do boring high school stuff, just like everyone else."

"Where's home for you?" Kellie asked Jemma. She'd made up her mind to join the group in the dining room so that she could get to know the visitor better. After all, they'd be working together on location.

"Baltimore," the actress replied. "We moved there after Mom and Dad split up. I was eight years old."

"Sorry," Kellie said gently.

"No, it's cool. And sorry if I keep on staring at you, but it is really weird how alike we are."

"I know. It feels like I'm looking in a mirror when I look at you, except your hair's a shade lighter."

"And your teeth are whiter."

"But your lashes are longer."

Jemma and Kellie cut short the comparisons and laughed.

"So how was Baltimore?" Kellie asked.

"Well, Mom had to work nights at the local store, so she sent me to after-school drama classes. I knew pretty soon that acting was what I wanted to do as a career. It's been my whole life for six years."

"So Jeb's movie is a big break for you. It must be really exciting." Kami compared it with how she felt when Lizzie picked her out to join Stardust Stables. That spring she'd been spotted in the county barrel racing contest. Before she knew it, she had joined the Stardust stunt-riding team.

"It is," Jemma agreed. "I can't wait till we start shooting."

"Which is when?" Kellie asked.

"A week from Saturday, unless —" Jemma frowned, then stopped suddenly.

"Unless what?" Hayley wanted to know.

"I probably shouldn't say . . ."

"Then don't," Alisa said, tactful and grown-up as always.

"No, tell us!" said Hayley.

"Unless Jeb has to change his schedule," Jemma finished. "Actually, there's a problem with funding for the movie — I heard him on the phone when we drove over here this morning. One of his business partners pulled out and took ten thousand dollars with him. The budget was already tight, and now shooting may not go ahead on time unless Jeb can find a new sponsor. I don't really understand the details. All I know is that Jeb sounded stressed."

"Everyone has money problems these days," Alisa said. Across the dining room she saw that Lizzie and Jack were sitting in a quiet corner with Jeb, away from the crowd. They were deep in conversation, with the director doing most of the talking.

Back at Jemma's table, the mood had grown more serious.

"Don't get me wrong — *Welcome the Wind*

will happen," Jemma said earnestly. "Jeb is totally committed to making the movie. He just has to look at ways of reducing costs and finding more money to make it work."

∽ ◦ ⌒

"What if he doesn't find the money?" Alisa wondered.

Jeb and Jemma had driven away in the old blue Jeep. Now Alisa and Kellie were busy in the tack room sorting, cleaning, and re-labeling bridles.

"Then I don't have a job after all and no one gets paid," Kellie said glumly. The excitement of the morning was gone and with it the feel-good factor of being chosen to work on the movie.

"I know. I hate all this uncertainty." Alisa rubbed hard to get a perfect sheen on Diabolo's metal bit before she hung it back on its hook.

"Hey!" Lizzie interrupted the gloomy talk by emerging from her office. "My door was open — I couldn't help overhearing."

Alisa and Kellie exchanged guilty looks. "Sorry. We heard that Jeb has a cash-flow problem," Alisa said.

"We talked about that over lunch," Lizzie explained calmly. "Jeb understands that Jack and I are in this business because we love what we do. He gets that it's not all about the money."

Except that it is, Kellie thought. She knew how badly Lizzie and Jack needed cash to keep the place running and to pay their young stunt riders a decent fee.

"So we agreed to be flexible," Lizzie went on. "I'm telling you this, Kellie, because you need to know that the job is definitely still there. Somehow Jack and I will find the money we need to pay you."

As she listened to Lizzie, Kellie felt her mood lift again and she smiled at Alisa.

"That's better!" Lizzie said. "Jack and I told Jeb we wouldn't take any payment for the stunt work on the film until his extra funding came through. That could be next week, next month, or next year. We trust him to pay us as soon as he can."

"So we still begin filming in nine days?" Kellie asked.

Lizzie nodded. "In Wyoming. Jeb and his location manager, Harry Ziegfeld, took up Hayley's advice and decided to shoot at Jackson

Hole. It's less than a day's drive from here. So you and I start work in the round pen tomorrow."

"That's so cool!" Alisa said excitedly. Hanging Diabolo's bridle on its hook, she hurried off to break the latest news to everyone.

"Like Alisa says — everything's cool, huh?" Lizzie asked Kellie.

"Yep." Kellie's heart beat fast and her cheeks flushed red. She had another big question for Lizzie but it was one she hardly dared to ask.

"You sure?" Lizzie prompted.

"Yep, cool."

"But?" Lizzie studied Kellie's face. "What's on your mind?"

"Nine days to learn the stunts?" Kellie checked again. "And what does the contract say? Does it say me and Legend, or . . . ?"

"Or?" At last Lizzie understood where this was going. She waited for Kellie to spit it out.

"Or me and Dylan?" Kellie was so stressed that she could hardly shape the words.

"It says Kellie Pryor. It doesn't mention any horse by name."

Kellie's eyes lit up and she gasped. "So it could be Dylan!"

Lizzie nodded slowly without taking her eyes

off Kellie. "Yes, if Dylan's leg is healed and if Jeb says it's okay."

"So you'll check with him?" Kellie urged. She pictured a fairy godmother waving her wand and making all her dreams come true!

"I will," Lizzie agreed, reaching for a rake that was propped against the wall. "You see this?"

Kellie nodded.

"You see those piles of poop?"

She nodded again, grinned, grabbed the rake, and without another word scooted out into the corral.

Chapter 6

"Kellie doesn't do patient," Tom said. "It doesn't come naturally to her."

It had been two days since his sister had successfully auditioned for the work on *Welcome the Wind,* and it seemed to him she couldn't sit still for even ten seconds.

"Look at her now," he told Kami as they sat on a rock by the creek, holding hands. It was early Friday evening and the sun was low in the sky, casting long shadows across the meadow where Kellie worked with Dylan. She was leading him around, walking him up and down to gently exercise the injured joint. "She spends every spare minute on that horse's rehab."

Kami was enjoying the peaceful scene. "I respect it!" she said. "I mean it, Tom. Kellie's made it her mission to get Dylan one hundred percent fit, and I admire her for it."

Tom wrinkled his nose.

"What?" Kami asked, nudging him with her elbow.

"That's all very well, but Lizzie didn't get a reply from Jeb yet."

"About which horse he wants to be in the movie?"

Tom nodded. "I guess he's busy chasing a new investor. Choosing between Legend and Dylan is not at the top of his to-do list."

"Poor Kellie — she'd be devastated if he picked Legend," Kami said. She remembered a tense conversation that the girls had had over breakfast that morning.

"Dylan's rehab is going well," Kellie had reported. "The infection has cleared up and luckily there's no long-term damage to the joint."

"So he's not lame any more?" Hayley had asked.

"A little stiff maybe."

"He still favors the other leg?"

"Not too much, but yeah — I guess a little," Kellie had replied, a bit of an edge creeping into her voice.

"What does Lizzie reckon — will he be okay to travel up to Jackson Hole?" Becca had asked as she stood up to clear the remnants of eggs and bacon from her breakfast plate into the trash can.

"That's if Jeb gives them the go-ahead," Alisa had reminded everyone.

"Jeez, you think I don't know that?" Kellie had snapped as she jumped up from the table and beat Becca to the trash. "Honestly, Alisa — you don't have to tell me what I already know!"

In the dim light of evening, Kami watched Kellie lead Dylan to the creek, her wavy hair blowing in the breeze. "You're right in one way, Tom — Kellie doesn't like to sit around," said Kami. "But when it comes to that horse's rehab, she's gentle and patient as can be."

Tom saw Dylan lower his head to drink while Kellie turned her face to gaze at the sun setting behind Clearwater Peak. "She loves him, that's why," he murmured, his fingers interlaced with Kami's. "I get that — I really do."

∾ ◦ ◡

While Dylan recuperated over the weekend, Kellie continued to ride Legend and work with Lizzie. They were working hard on the big stunt that they would need for the climactic scene in *Welcome the Wind*. There was still no word from Jeb on which horse he wanted, but in the meanwhile there was plenty to do.

"Okay, so Jemma's character has a major scene involving an accident with her horse," Lizzie explained to Kellie on the Sunday afternoon. "It's 1932 and her family is on the move. They've finished a job on the Triple Diamond cattle ranch, and now they have to move west to California to look for more work."

"But Martha doesn't want to leave." Kellie had also read the script. "She's worked with a ranch horse called Sacramento. They have a special bond, and she doesn't want to say goodbye."

Lizzie nodded as Kellie mounted Legend. "So she sneaks out with Sacramento late at night for one last ride. There's no moon, so it's pretty dark. She takes him out through the lot where the rancher is holding five hundred head of cattle, ready for market. A ranch hand drives by and mistakes Martha for a rustler. He fires a warning shot. Sacramento spooks, runs at the fence, and jumps it, right into the path of the vehicle."

"So it has to look as if my horse crashes into the truck." Kellie ran through the sequence in her mind. "Timing is going to be pretty important."

"Which is why we practice it here before you get on the set. Obviously we don't have five hundred head of cattle and we don't have a 1930s-style truck, but this is the fence I want you to jump and that's the position the truck will be in." Lizzie pointed to the tractor they used for trailering muck out of the corral. It was the same vehicle they'd used in the round pen to get the horses accustomed to the sound of a noisy engine.

Kellie took in the information. "It'll be moving toward us as we jump, right? How fast?"

"Real slow — under ten miles per hour. Tomorrow I'll get Tom to drive the truck at that speed. But first let's teach Legend to spook, then jump the fence, and fall. That'll do for a start."

"Okay, so Sacramento goes down. The script says the truck hits him and he falls on top of his rider. Ouch!" Kellie pictured the painful end to the sequence.

"Don't worry — you know the cameras can fake that. For now I want you to let Legend land, fall and roll onto his side, and lie there without moving. In other words, he plays dead."

"Okay, let's see if he can do it." Dylan was a good play-dead horse, but until now Kellie had never tried the stunt with Legend. Timing was everything — she had to kick free and leap clear as she rolled, and he had to understand that he couldn't get up until Kellie gave him the word.

After checking Legend's cinch, Lizzie gave the signal for the rehearsal to begin.

Kellie rode around the pen to settle her horse then steered him toward the fence. She waited for Lizzie to give a loud clap to imitate the gunshot, then she sent the Palomino into a spectacular rearing action. The rearing was followed by big crow hops sideways toward the fence, then a sudden twist and jerk up and over the rails. The second she felt him plunge down on the far side, Kellie got ready to bail.

"Now!" Lizzie called urgently.

Kellie kicked hard with her right heel to send Legend reeling to his left, throwing him so far off balance that Legend's knees gave way and he rolled in the dirt.

At the same time, Kellie slipped her feet free of the stirrups and flung herself off to the right, landing safely in time to see Legend go down and roll onto his side.

But would he stay down? Kellie held her breath.

"Whoa!" Lizzie said as a surprised Legend

scrambled up immediately. He shook himself from head to foot then trotted toward the gate.

"Come back!" Kellie called.

But Legend had spotted Tom, Ross, and Kami hosing down saddle blankets in the corral. The gate to the round pen was open, and he headed through it toward what looked like fun with the water hose.

"Come back, Legend! We need to do that all over again!" Kellie cried.

He ignored her and trotted right on to join Tom and the others.

"Hmm," Lizzie frowned and tipped her hat to the back of her head. "I can see this stunt still needs a lot of work."

∽ ◦ ꙮ

"You know what they say — you wait all day for a bus to come then three arrive at once," Jack yelled excitedly as he entered the corral at a run. He grinned from ear to ear, waving an email that he'd just printed out.

"Whoa, wait, catch your breath!" Tom said as Jack came to a stop.

It was late Monday afternoon and Tom, Kami,

Ross, Alisa, Becca, and Zak were preparing to set out on a leisurely, after-work trail ride.

"What's up?" Zak asked.

"We just got a request for three stunt riders! It's from the New Moon movie company. Three!" Jack repeated with happy emphasis.

"That's crazy," Becca said. "Do we know who, what, why . . . ?"

"Three riders," Jack repeated. "They're making a horse-whisperer-type blockbuster. They need two girls and one guy."

"Where?" asked Kami.

"Connecticut. And they need them this Thursday."

"That's awesome," Alisa said. Along with Tom, Zak, Ross, Kami, and Becca, plus Kellie and Hayley, who had come out of the barn to see what the fuss was about, she hoped to be chosen as one of the three. *Oh wait — not Kellie,* she thought. *She's already got the* Welcome the Wind *work.* This upped her own chances a little bit.

"We have Lizzie to thank for this," Jack said. "She's been on the phone non-stop looking for work. It turns out that New Moon was let down by another stunt-riding outfit at the last minute. That's why they need us so soon."

"So who gets to go?" Becca asked. A horse-whisperer movie would be cool to work on.

"It was Lizzie's decision." Jack paused to read from the email. "There was no time for auditions, so she offered three names and New Moon accepted them. The names are . . . Becca, Kami, and Ross!"

"Woo!" the others chorused.

Ross high-fived Kami and Becca, who grinned back at him. Connecticut sounded like a cool place to be.

"Sorry you weren't on the list," Kellie whispered to Hayley while the other girls celebrated.

Hayley shrugged. "Lizzie has her reasons," she insisted. She had a sudden thought that made her grin. "Hey, I get to stay here and hang out with Tom and Zak — what's so hard about that?"

"And your name will be on the top of the list next time for sure."

"I hope so." Secretly, Hayley did mind that she hadn't been included yet again. In fact, it really hurt. "Have a great ride," she called across the corral to the group of happy riders as they set out along the Jeep trail.

Hayley and Kellie were working on stacking

hay bales onto the trailer when Jack came looking for Kellie.

"I have more news," he told her, his face blank of any expression.

Kellie and Hayley stared at him eagerly.

"Finally, we heard from Jeb Burns."

Kellie tried to read his face but failed. "And?" she asked, her heart thumping against her ribs.

"He thought about the choice we offered — Legend or Dylan. Kind of Beauty and the Beast, we told him."

Kellie sprang to Dylan's defense. "Hey, that's not fair — Dylan's just as cute as Legend!"

"He's kidding," Hayley whispered.

"So he knew he had to choose between a Palomino he'd already seen in action, or a dark bay he hadn't . . ."

"Jeez, Jack! Just tell me!" Kellie begged.

"Well, Jeb said he trusted our knowledge of the two horses. But were we sure they were both suitable for the big scene involving the truck accident?" Jack strung out the suspense for as long as he could. "And you know Lizzie — when Jeb asked her the direct question, she had to be completely honest."

Hayley stepped forward to end Kellie's

misery. "So whose name did she say? Come on, Jack, spit it out."

"Dylan," he said. "Be happy, Kellie. So long as you put in the work in the round pen with him, you get to take your own beautiful boy to Wyoming!"

Chapter 7

The following day saw the start of full-on action in the round pen at Stardust.

While Kellie and Dylan focused on practicing for their up-and-coming stunt work on *Welcome the Wind*, Jack took charge of working with Ross, Becca, and Kami for the New Moon project in Connecticut.

"Who here needs a refresher course on natural horsemanship?" he asked them, readying them for their new contract.

Kami's hand went up. "I guess I know the basics, but I'd appreciate a few reminders."

"Becca, can you help her out?" Jack asked.

"It's all about trust between horse and rider," came the prompt reply. "And about the rider always seeing things from the horse's point of view."

"Right on," Jack nodded. "You get your horse

to trust you and you don't violate that trust — not ever!"

Kami hung on to every word, absorbing Jack's expert knowledge.

"Listen to me," he went on. "I've trained a lot of horses and riders over the years. Whenever people come to me and tell me they have a problem with their horse, my job is to turn it around and allow them to see that I don't help people with horse problems, I help horses with people problems!"

Kami grinned. "Horses with people problems. I like that." Like anyone who spent time in stable yards and corrals, she came across plenty of nervous riders who communicated their tension to their horses — who then got skittish and unpredictable themselves. Or people who used spurs or a whip to get extra speed out of a tired horse without realizing that every equine, no matter how strong and willing, needs a break and time to catch their breath.

"And I'm always against using force as a training method," Jack went on. "Just keep in mind one word — 'never.' That's it, end of story."

"Jack is such a cool trainer!" Becca murmured to Kami. "This is why we love him."

"So the plotline for the New Moon movie revolves around a situation where a rich city guy gets enough money to buy a ranch in New England, complete with stables and horses for his city-slicker guests to ride. Only, he hires the wrong type of trainer to bring on his colts — an old-fashioned guy who uses cruel methods on the horses behind the owner's back. So naturally the colts develop trust issues. They spook real easily or they try bucking their novice riders off. You get the picture. It takes a junior on the yard to spot what the problem is and put it right. He's the hero of the movie."

"And we play the role of city slickers?" Ross asked. "We get bucked off and so on?"

"Exactly."

"I'm cool with that," Becca said. "Those stunts sound like they should be pretty straightforward."

Nevertheless, Jack insisted on intensive training with Legend, Magic, and Pepper before the group left. This meant that Lizzie had less time to train Kellie and Dylan in the round pen.

"But that's okay," Lizzie told Kellie as she rode Dylan into the pen for his first training session since his injury. "We'll take things nice and easy — see how his leg holds up."

This feels so good! Kellie thought. Her dream had come true — she was back with Dylan! She smiled at Hayley, who sat astride the gate, texting home to her mom in Jackson Hole.

"Let's start with easy rein work," Lizzie decided. "I want a slow, counterclockwise lope for a full circuit. Then break into a fast lope for one circuit, then slow again. Alternate until I ask you to stop."

Yeah, nice and easy! Kellie worked Dylan into his slow lope. "He feels balanced," she called to Hayley. "How does he look?"

"Good," Hayley replied, slipping her phone into her pocket. She was still trying hard not to mind being left out of the Connecticut job. "Really, Kellie — he looks amazing!"

"Now lope clockwise. This time, put in a couple of flying lead changes," Lizzie instructed. "And finish with a sliding stop."

Nothing complicated. Kellie beamed with pride as Dylan executed the lead changes perfectly and kicked up dirt on his sliding stop. "What do you think? Is he ready to put in some spins?"

"Just a couple to test out the leg," Lizzie told her. "Then we'll finish for today."

Okay, buddy — hindquarter spin! Kellie leaned forward and brought her knees up, pressing against Dylan's withers with her right knee — the signal for him to lower his haunches and turn counterclockwise on the spot. She knew it looked spectacular when a thousand pounds of bone and muscle spun so quickly.

"Good boy!" Dylan came out of the spin and a delighted Kellie reached forward to pat his neck. "That was perfect."

"Tomorrow we'll build up to the big play-dead scene," Lizzie promised. "Then we'll give him a day off on Thursday before trailering him out to Jackson Hole on Friday."

∽ ◦ ᕋ

Once they were done for the day, Alisa, Kellie, Kami, Hayley, and Becca spent their evenings doing laundry. Then, while the washers and driers were busy, they would catch up with friends and family by Twitter, text, and email.

All good here, Kellie texted home to her parents in Colorado Springs. *Dylan's leg is okay. Friday we trailer him out to Wyoming.* The message was followed by six smiley faces.

Hayley received a text from her mom. *U OK? U seemed sad earlier.*

She texted back. *A little homesick, maybe. But fine, thanks.*

"Are these my jeans, or yours?" Becca asked Kami, pulling clothes out of a shared machine.

"Mine." Kami recognized the faded, frayed patches on the knees.

Quieter than usual, Hayley hovered in the doorway and eventually drifted off for a solo stroll by the creek.

∾ ◦ ☙

The next day, Hayley was hanging out on the tack-room porch when Lizzie sought her out.

"What's up?" Lizzie asked.

"Nothing. I'm good." Hayley had just walked Cool Kid out to the meadow and was taking a break before she joined the others in the house for dinner. She had resigned herself to staying back at Stardust with Zak and Tom while the others worked.

"You're a terrible liar, Hayley. Did you know that?" Lizzie noted.

"What do you mean?"

"Your face is an open book. You're not feeling good at all, are you?"

Hayley sighed then shrugged.

"So . . . do you want to drive with Kellie and me to Wyoming and be our navigator?" Lizzie said after a long, thoughtful pause.

"Me?"

"Yes, you. You're not saying no to a long weekend with your parents, are you?"

"You're giving me time off to see my family?"

"Three days, that's all. You plan the route for us and we drop you off Friday evening in Jackson Hole. We pick you up early Tuesday to drive back to Stardust."

Hayley didn't have to think about it for more than a second. "You bet!" she said with a grin. She ran ahead to the dining room to tell the others.

Chapter 8

On Thursday morning it was Tom, not Hayley, who was moping around the tack room.

"Don't tell me — Kami left without saying goodbye!" Zak teased when he caught Tom leaning on his broom, staring into space. "Dude, how in the world will you survive without her for five whole days?"

Tom didn't answer. Instead he retaliated by sweeping a cloud of dust over Zak's newly cleaned cowboy boots and then tripping him with the end of the brush. Zak toppled against the row of halters, pulling Tom with him. Kellie found them there, tangled up among the lead ropes. She called for Hayley to join her as a witness to the stupidity of her brother and of boys in general.

"Would you look at this mess," she said. She folded her arms and leaned against the doorpost.

"They're the ones who'll have to clean it up," Hayley pointed out.

"And you thought it'd be fun to hang out with these guys," Kellie said with a shake of her head.

"Yeah, look what I'm missing."

Kellie and Hayley's scorn made no difference; Tom and Zak wrestled on regardless.

∽ ◦ ℃

There was a strict routine for trailering horses out of Stardust. It involved cleaning the horse's tack and storing it in the trailer cab the evening before an early morning start, plus laying a straw bed in the back of the trailer, filling hay nets, and finally getting an adult to check the tire pressure and gas for the journey ahead. On the day itself, usually before dawn, the rider got up and brought in his or her horse from the meadow to groom him until he gleamed. Then the rider strapped on a tail bandage and padded leg protectors.

The horse would know what all this was leading to — a long drive and work at the end of it. So he would stay alert as the trainer worked, pawing the ground as if to say, *"Let's go!"*

"We won't be long," Kellie promised Dylan as she tethered him to a rail. Then she and Hayley went off for an early Friday morning breakfast.

But it turned out she was too wound up to eat, so Hayley made peanut butter and jelly sandwiches and took granola bars from the kitchen for later. At seven-thirty exactly, they went back to the corral and found Lizzie loading Dylan into the trailer.

By eight, Lizzie, Hayley, Kellie, and Dylan were on the interstate, heading to Wyoming.

∾ ◦ ୯౿

They hit Jackson Hole with the sun setting over the Grand Tetons, after a day of singing along to country and Western music on the radio.

"Take a left," Hayley told Lizzie when they came to the first traffic light they'd seen in ages. "My folks bought a convenience store on Whitewater Road after Mom retired from stunt riding. Drive a little farther . . . okay, we're here!"

Lizzie pulled up and let the engine idle. "Enjoy your mini-break," she told Hayley. "And who knows what work we may find for you before the end of the summer . . ."

"You think?" Hayley asked as she jumped down and looked up hopefully at Lizzie.

"Anything's possible," Lizzie insisted. "And remember, Hayley — you're a great rider."

A bright smile flashed across Hayley's face as she said her goodbyes and ran across the street. Lizzie waited until Hayley's dad appeared at the door to greet his daughter.

"See you Tuesday!" Kellie called.

Then Lizzie and Kellie were back on the road for the last thirty-minute stretch to Molly Gulch, the location for *Welcome the Wind*. Jeb had described it as being "in the middle of nowhere." He wasn't lying.

"Tired?" Lizzie asked a yawning Kellie as they followed a narrow road winding up into the mountains. Pine trees on either side of the road cast deep shadows, with glimpses of a stunning mountain range rising out of the flat plain below.

Kellie nodded. "You?"

"Yep, but we're almost there. As soon as we arrive we'll show Dylan to his living quarters then we can get some sleep — which will be under canvas, by the way."

"You mean we're camping?"

"Yeah, the budget for this movie is tiny,

remember." A wooden sign ahead pointed them down a dirt road to Molly Gulch.

Kellie held tight as the trailer bumped along the rutted track. "Excellent!" she said with a smile. "I love camping out under the stars."

"Just as well," Lizzie said. "There are no fancy beds and heated towel racks on this job. I guarantee it!"

∽ ◦ ∾

And no movie-star tantrums from the leading lady, either — Kellie understood this the moment they opened up the trailer to unload Dylan.

"Hey, guys!" Dressed in jeans and a T-shirt, Jemma ran to greet them with broad smiles and hugs. "So good to see you. I've been waiting all day for you to get here."

While Lizzie went to find Jeb in the catering tent, Jemma led Kellie and Dylan to a small meadow overlooked on all sides by tall pinyon pines and smaller, silver-barked aspens. To make it secure, the area was fenced off with slim plastic posts and electric tape.

"There's no creek here, so I filled three buckets of water for him — that's enough, isn't it?" said Jemma, standing by the gate while Kellie led Dylan into the compound.

"Plenty." And looking around at the lush grass, Kellie decided that Dylan would be fine as far as food went. "I guess I'll pitch my tent under that tree so I can keep a close eye on him."

Jemma nodded. "Good idea. Come with me and I'll show you the girls' shower block. Then you can grab something to eat."

"I already said goodnight to Lizzie, so just point me to the restroom and show me where I can find a tent and a sleeping bag." Kellie was eager to get back to Dylan. She pulled out the peanut butter and jelly sandwiches that Hayley had made. They were squished out of shape after a whole day in Kellie's bag. "This is all I want right now."

"Yuck!" Jemma made a disgusted face then giggled.

"Here's the guy we need," she said after Kellie had visited the bathroom. A short, young-looking man in glasses came down the metal steps of one of the white trucks containing technical equipment. He stopped and did a double take when he saw the similarity between Jemma and Kellie.

"Harry, this is Kellie Pryor, my stunt-riding double," Jemma explained. "Kellie, meet Harry Ziegfeld — he's our location manager. Kellie needs a one-man tent and a sleeping bag."

"Coming up!" Harry replied, disappearing back inside the truck and returning with the goods. "Anything else you need, just let me know."

By this time Kellie was almost too tired to walk in a straight line. "Sorry, I'm no fun," she yawned at Jemma. She thanked Harry and took the tent and sleeping bag from him.

"No, I understand — you need sleep," said Jemma, taking the hint. "I'm super glad you're here. I'll see you tomorrow." Smiling, she watched Kellie make her way back to her chosen camping spot.

Luckily the tent was the lightweight kind you can pitch by tossing it in the air. It was ready within seconds.

"Hey, Dylan, what's up?" Kellie whispered to her horse, who had come right up to the electric tape.

He lowered his head and nickered.

"You came to say goodnight, huh?" She went to give her horse a quick hug. As she stood with her arms wrapped around him, she glanced up at the myriad of stars in the clear sky. *To infinity and beyond*, she thought. "Perfect," she said.

Then, with Dylan watching, she crawled into the little blue tent, zipped up her sleeping bag, and closed her eyes.

Chapter 9

Early next morning, Jeb set up lights, microphones, and cameras before giving Kellie instructions for the scene he was about to shoot.

"Your character, Martha, rides her horse into that bunch of willows by the creek," he told her. "There's a calf in there that got separated from her mom, and Martha's on a mission to find her."

Kellie listened carefully. "Is the calf in position already?" she asked.

"Yep. We have a production assistant hidden in there with her. He'll release her when I give the signal, then you ride into the bushes to drive her out into the open. She'll be hollering for her mom, so you'll have no problem finding her."

"What do you want Dylan and me to do once she's out of the willows?"

"You should head her downhill to make it look like you're driving her to catch up with the rest of the herd. Think you can do that in one take?" Jeb had spent a lot of time giving Kellie the complete picture, but he was glancing anxiously at his watch. He was doing his best to keep to a tight schedule.

"Sure we can," she promised.

So Jeb called for action, and the cameras started rolling.

"Let's go," Kellie whispered to Dylan, who already had the calf's scent in his nostrils. She pointed her horse toward the willows, looking for signs of life. Sure enough, she could see the slender branches moving and hear the leaves rustling. Then the captive calf let out a high, lost cry. Kellie steered Dylan toward the sound. "Take it nice and easy," she told him, leaving him on a loose rein to find his own way into the thicket.

Dylan ducked his head and plowed boldly through the willows. Kellie hunched low in the saddle and slowly pushed aside the wispy branches.

There was a loud rustle and a lowing sound, and then the production assistant released the black calf. It stood in front of Kellie and Dylan, staring wildly around.

Dylan froze, eyeballing the frightened calf and waiting for his next instruction.

"Okay, we're not rushing this," Kellie decided. "We're going to ease around behind her and drive her out so that she's pointing downhill."

Cautiously, Dylan stepped through the willows, giving the calf a wide berth until Kellie was happy with their line of attack. "Now!" she urged.

Dylan lunged at the bewildered calf. He nudged her hindquarters with his nose, until she stopped wailing and shot out of the bushes right where Jeb had wanted her. Kellie and Dylan were on her tail, pushing her down the hill, steering her back on track when she threatened to flee off to the side. This involved some athletic stops and sharp turns from Dylan, which he executed directly in front of the nearest camera. His timing and positioning couldn't have been more perfect.

"Good boy," Kellie said. "You're the best cow horse in the business!"

"Great job!" Jeb cried from his vantage point on top of a nearby rock. "Excellent work. Cut!"

∽⊙∾

"This next scene involves close-ups of Jemma and her horse," Jeb explained to Kellie.

The crew had eaten lunch and taken up position outside an old red barn chosen by Harry to evoke the dusty, tumbleweed days of the 1930s Depression. Set against the spectacular Teton mountains, with its rusting iron roof and log walls, the front of the barn was hung with sets of deer and elk antlers, weather-beaten and whitened by age. It made a perfect frame for the intimate scene between Martha and Sacramento.

"Kellie, I want you to place your horse in the entrance to the barn and ask him to stay there. There's no stunt work involved, so you don't feature in the actual scene this time — but I need you on hand in case Dylan gets distracted and tries to walk away."

"Okay." Feeling a little deflated after the morning's high-octane activity, Kellie edged him into position. "I know," she whispered in his ear. "This isn't as fun as working with cattle but what can I say, except, 'Mister Dylan, it's time for your close-up!'"

Dylan tossed his dark mane and shuffled impatiently. "Don't move an inch — stay right there!" Kellie instructed as she stepped out of sight. She climbed a straw bale inside the barn and peeped through a horizontal chink in the wall.

"Action!" Jeb called.

Dylan stood in the doorway looking at Jemma as she walked toward him. With ears pricked and dark mane flopping forward, he looked incredibly cute. The sun shone on Jemma's face, its light dancing in her gray eyes. A wisp of hair escaped from one of her braids and blew across her cheek as she reached up to stroke Dylan's nose. She placed the flat of her hand against his neck. Dylan dipped his head with perfect timing, allowing Jemma to kiss the top of his nose.

"Cut!" Jeb called.

∽ ◦ ⌒

"What's eating you?" Lizzie asked a glum-looking Kellie during the afternoon break from filming. They were sitting with cold drinks outside the catering tent, taking care to stay in the shade of a tree and out of the sun's heat.

"You should be happy — Jemma is really friendly, and Dylan is doing a magnificent job."

"I know," Kellie said with a sigh. "She is. He is. You're right."

"But?" Lizzie urged.

"No, nothing — honestly." Kellie got up and chucked her empty paper cup into the trash. "Sorry, I have to get into costume for the next scene."

"You have plenty of time," Lizzie pointed out. She frowned a little as Kellie walked off.

"Everything okay?" Jeb stopped to ask, phone glued to his ear and script tucked under his arm.

"I think so." Lizzie looked doubtful until suddenly a light went off in her head. "Oh, I get it!" she exclaimed.

"Get what?"

"What's eating Kellie. It's Jemma and Dylan. They bonded big-time during the barn scene. Now Kellie's green with envy!"

∽ ◦ ❤

"Kellie Pryor, get over yourself." Out in the grassy clearing with Dylan, Kellie gave herself a stern talking-to. "Dylan, we all know you're totally gorgeous. So of course Jemma fell in love with you — how could she not?"

Lowering his head to grab a mouthful of grass, Dylan seemed to suggest that he didn't know what had got into her. He munched contentedly and let her talk.

"I know I'm being mean, but I can't help it," Kellie said with a sigh, brushing a stray wisp of hay from the bib of her Depression-era overalls. The rest of her costume was made up of a shapeless straw hat, faded red shirt, and dirty canvas shoes with rope soles. "We're meant to be the team here. You and me. Not you and Jemma."

Dylan tore up another clump of juicy grass with his big front teeth and munched on.

"You're right. I need to stop feeling this way and focus on our next stunt," she decided, going to fetch Dylan's saddle.

"We're working with more cattle this evening," she told him when she came back with his saddle, lifting it onto his back. "Time to show everyone what we can do — again."

∽ ◦ ໑

This scene took place in the pen behind the red barn. At around one hundred square feet, it was crowded with jostling cattle. It was also slick underfoot with fresh cow pies — hot and extremely smelly.

"And I bet you thought stunt riding was glamorous," Kellie quipped to Jemma, who had come to watch her and Dylan.

"It's the same with acting," Jemma replied. "Not many people know how much hanging around in costume and makeup trailers is involved."

"Plus learning lines and waiting on set," Kellie agreed. "I could never be an actor!"

"And I could never do what you do — it's too dangerous." As she talked, Jemma used her cell phone's camera to take pictures of Kellie and Dylan. "Is it okay if I record the run-through of this next stunt?"

"Go ahead," Kellie told her. She was over the spike of jealousy she'd felt earlier that day and was ready for action. "Are you sure you're okay to be out here?" she asked. "You look a little pale."

"I'm fine," Jemma assured her, holding her phone at arm's length.

"So, Kellie, choose any cow you like out of this bunch," Jeb said from his director's chair. "You box him in against the fence in the near corner and then run him along the fence toward the chute over there to our right. Got that?"

Kellie replied with a cheerful nod and a thumbs-up.

"We're not filming this time — this is a rehearsal so I can decide exactly where to set up cameras," he reminded her. "I want you to include some tight turns and circles, and some sliding stops that you can repeat for the real thing. Can you do that?"

"Yeah, gotcha," Kellie said above the deep bellows of the livestock that surrounded her. She picked out a young black steer and began threading her way quietly through the herd. Dylan went about his work, cutting the steer off from his buddies and pushing him up against the fence. The steer ducked his head and looked set to charge, but Dylan didn't flinch. Instead, he darted at the steer, sending him running down the length of the fence.

"Yee-hah!" Lifting the battered straw hat from her head, Kellie waved it in the air and gave an ear-splitting cowgirl yell. Then she added two more sprints and a couple of sliding stops for good measure.

The steer came to the entrance of the chute, hesitated, then trotted in good as gold, out into a holding pen at the far end.

"Thank you, Kellie. Thank you, Dylan!" Jeb yelled, obviously excited by what he'd seen.

Feeling satisfied with the rehearsal take, Kellie started riding back to join the director. She passed Jemma on her way over. "Did you get that on video?" she asked excitedly.

"Yeah, it was so cool. I'm going to put it on YouTube. Soon you'll have thousands of new fans!" Jemma promised. "Whoa!" Jemma lost her balance, catching herself just in time. As she leaned against the fence, she fumbled and almost dropped her phone in the mud inside the pen.

"Are you sure you're okay?" Kellie asked.

"Fine — just a little dizzy, that's all."

"Really? You don't look fine." Kellie noticed that Jemma's face was even paler than before. There were beads of sweat on her forehead and her denim shirt had dark patches under the arms.

"I'm fine, honestly." Pushing herself upright, Jemma took a deep breath and began walking uncertainly toward the costume trailer parked beside the old barn.

Kellie frowned, ignoring Jeb's request to join him. "Watch out!" she yelled as Jemma paused, then swayed. "Quick, someone! She needs help!"

It was too late. Waves of heat shimmered up from the dusty track, and Kellie watched powerlessly as Jemma's knees buckled and she fell to the ground.

Chapter 10

"Jemma probably stayed out in the direct sunlight for too long yesterday," Lizzie said. "I'd say she has sunstroke."

She and Kellie were up early on Sunday morning, eager to put in some last-minute training on Dylan's play-dead trick, a climactic nighttime scene that Jeb wanted to shoot soon after the sun went down.

Kellie was still worried. "She looked pretty sick. Harry and Ellie, a girl from the costume department, they had to pick her up out of the dirt and carry her to the first-aid tent. The last I heard, Jeb had called a doctor in Jackson Hole."

"I'm sure she'll be fine," Lizzie assured her. "So, are we going to rehearse this stunt or not?"

Kellie nodded and led the way into Dylan's paddock. "Look at the gorgeous boy. See how lazy and laid back he is?"

Dylan barely raised his head when Lizzie and Kellie approached. Instead, he kept on eating and swishing away flies with his tail. "Grass, water, plenty of shade from the aspens — he's in his element," Lizzie agreed. "But we should put in an hour's training with him before the sun gets too hot. Sorry, old guy, you have to come with us."

"Hey, he's only twelve," Kellie protested as Lizzie fastened a halter on him. "He's in his prime."

Lizzie smiled. "Whatever," she replied as she led Dylan slowly out of the paddock.

The three of them ambled along the dirt track, past the pen holding the cattle. "This is the fence you'll jump when the gunshot spooks him," Lizzie pointed out, scuffing the ground with the toe of her boot. "You land right here."

Kellie noted the spot. "Gotcha. Let's get him saddled up and working — like you said, the temperature will soar before we know it."

By the time they'd saddled Dylan, other people were starting to go about their different jobs.

"Hey, Kellie. Hey, Lizzie," Ellie called as she hurried up the steps into the costume trailer.

A sound man carried coils of cable into the barn. Jeb came out of the catering tent and walked quickly to his blue Jeep.

"Hey, Jeb — how's Jemma?" Kellie called after him, but he was too caught up in a phone conversation to reply.

"Ready?" Lizzie asked, checking Dylan's cinch, then holding his right stirrup steady as Kellie mounted from the other side.

Harry ran by with more cables. "Harry, how's Jemma?" Kellie yelled. "Is she any better?"

The location manager stopped and turned. "No, we've got a problem, actually."

Kellie gave a grunt of surprise. "What do you mean — is she still sick?"

He nodded. "The doctor came. She said it wasn't just sunstroke."

"So what is it?"

"She's not sure — maybe the effects of the heat combined with food poisoning or a virus. They took Jemma into town, and they're currently running some tests. Anyway, she's not able to work today, and Jeb is tearing his hair out."

"Poor Jemma," Kellie muttered. She asked Dylan to follow Lizzie, who was already heading toward the crowded livestock pen.

"Yeah, let's hope that she gets well soon," Lizzie said.

"Shouldn't we go and visit her, or send a card or something?"

"Nice idea — and we can definitely send a text. But right now we need to focus on what they've hired us to do." Lizzie held open the gate to let Kellie and Dylan into the pen. "This is the first time we've tried this stunt with actual cattle, so we'll start with the moment when the gun goes off and Dylan spooks."

Kellie and Dylan slowly threaded their way through the jostling cows. "What's the signal?" she yelled to Lizzie, who drew a gun out of her jacket pocket.

"This is a starter's pistol — it shoots blanks. Wait for me to fire it." She held it high over her head, pointing skyward.

Bang! The gun let out a single, loud crack.

As startled cows scattered in all directions, Kellie sat back sharply, thrust her legs forward in the stirrups, and pulled Dylan's reins tight. Up he went, rearing high and pawing the air. Quickly Kellie grabbed the saddle horn and hung on to it as he crashed down, rocked forward, then reared up again among the fleeing cattle.

"Good — good! It's going to look great on camera," Lizzie called from the track.

Kellie nodded and shifted her weight forward, a signal for Dylan to stop rearing. It was then that she noticed Jeb walking quickly to join Lizzie. He spoke and gestured toward Kellie. She saw Lizzie shake her head, and Jeb spoke again.

"Hey, Kellie, would you come over here a second?" Lizzie called.

She rode Dylan to the fence.

"Jeb has a question for you."

"Kellie, you know that Jemma's sick?" Jeb asked. He looked stressed.

She nodded and wondered what was coming next.

"She's spending the day at the doctor's house in Jackson Hole, where there's air conditioning, a decent shower, and everything she needs to get better fast."

"That's good," Kellie said while Dylan thrust his head over the fence. "Do they know what the problem is?"

"Probably a mixture of sunstroke and food poisoning — something she ate yesterday afternoon. A worker in the kitchen also went down with a gastric problem."

"Not good," Kellie said.

"Anyway, I was telling Lizzie — this throws our shooting schedule off big time. I mean, we have a real crisis on our hands."

"Every lost hour costs the production company money," Lizzie explained. "No way can the budget handle an extra day on location."

"I get that," Kellie said cautiously.

"So I was wondering . . ." Jeb slowed down and turned to Lizzie for help.

"He asked me if you had any acting experience," Lizzie finished. "I told him I didn't know."

"So do you?" Jeb asked, holding his breath as he waited for Kellie's answer.

"No. Zilch. Nada. Nothing." Kellie couldn't have been plainer. Like she'd told Jemma when they first met on set, she could never become an actor and the very idea of standing in front of a camera and spouting dialogue sent her pulse racing.

"No experience in high school musicals, for instance?" pressed Jeb.

"Nope, can't sing a note, can't dance a step," she insisted. "I have two left feet — ask my brother. Ask anyone."

"Well, luckily there's no singing or dancing involved. What about in middle school — did you ever take part in any Christmas productions?"

"Yeah — angels in Nativity plays, I guess. Non-speaking parts."

Jeb sighed. "Help me out here, Kellie. I'm a desperate man. I wouldn't be asking you to stand in for Jemma if I hadn't exhausted all other possibilities."

"You're asking me to stand in for Jemma?" Kellie echoed. "Whoa — I mean, whoa!"

"Just in one short scene with Matt, her screen brother," Jeb explained. "Martha and Matt argue about having to leave Sacramento behind while the family piles in the old truck and travels on, looking for grape-picking work in California. If you agree to double for Jemma, we can manipulate the camera angles so that it's not obvious you're a stand-in. We can also record Jemma's saying the lines and add them in later."

"So you won't be heard in the edited version," Lizzie said. "It's just your face and your body."

"Because, you must realize — there's a striking resemblance," Jeb pleaded. "I think we can get away with it. What do you say?"

Actual acting! Stunt riding — no problem. Put

me on a horse and I'll perform any trick you ask. But acting! Kellie took a deep breath.

"Well?" Lizzie prompted.

"Give me thirty minutes," Kellie replied.

∽ ◦ ∾

"Tom, it's me." Kellie sat inside her small blue tent and spoke urgently into her phone. "Guess what happened."

"What am I, a mind reader all of a sudden?" Her brother was in the corral at Stardust, hoping for a call from Kami in Connecticut. When Kellie's number showed on his phone, he was disappointed and didn't exactly try to hide it.

"Listen," she said. "Jemma Scott is sick. They want to use me as a stand-in to act her part."

"Ha, very funny!" Tom said.

This was exactly the reaction Kellie had expected. "Yeah, you said it. I tried to tell Jeb I can't act, but he doesn't believe me. What am I going to do?"

"Say no?" Tom suggested.

"Yeah, but if I don't do it, Jeb will have to re-write the schedule for shooting *Welcome the Wind* and there isn't any money in the budget to allow for that." She was desperate to get out of this, but when she heard Tom telling her not to do it, she started to feel bad.

"Then say yes."

"But, duh — I can't act, remember." They were back to square one. "In the scene they want me to do, the Martha character has an argument with her brother, Matt. I have to learn dialogue, make it look authentic and everything!"

"Your character fights with her brother?" Tom laughed again. "That's not acting, that's reality."

"How come?" Kellie asked, hunched miserably inside her hot tent.

"Because you fight with me in real life every day," he joked. "Go ahead and say yes, Kell — I know you can do it!"

∽ ◦ ∾

"Jemma? It's me, Kellie." It took a second phone conversation for Kellie to finally make up her mind. She'd got Jemma's number from Harry and instead of texting a get-well message, she made a call.

"Hey, Kellie." Jemma's voice sounded weak and shaky.

"How are you doing?"

"Okay," came the weary reply. "At least I've stopped needing to visit the bathroom every five minutes! Sorry, that's too much information, huh?"

"No, and I'm glad you're feeling better. When can you get back to work?"

"Soon, I hope. The doctor says the effects of this type of food poisoning should wear off after twenty-four hours. So if I take it easy, I can be on set again tomorrow. When do you and Dylan leave?"

"Early Tuesday."

"So I'll see you before you go."

"Yeah. Listen, Jemma, the other reason I'm calling is that I wanted to run an idea past you."

"Go ahead."

"You know how identical everyone says we are?" Kellie hesitated then quickly blurted everything out. "Well, today, while you're sick, Jeb wants me to stand in for you in the fight scene with your on-screen brother. What do you think?"

"You mean, am I okay with that?" Jemma asked.

"Yeah. And really, do you think I can do

it, even though I've never acted before?" It was hot and muggy in the zipped up tent, so Kellie crawled out to breathe cooler air. She saw Dylan quietly grazing in the green, sunny pasture, and the sight calmed her. "It'll be your voice they use, by the way — they'll lip-sync it in later."

"Who cares about that, anyway?" Jemma sounded thoughtful. "Listen, I can tell you what I think, but in the end you're the only one who can decide."

"I know." Kellie sighed. In the distance she saw Jeb step out of the trailer containing cameras and sound equipment. He headed purposefully in her direction.

"But I'll say one thing," Jemma said after a long pause. "If you decide to do it, remember you'll be doing it not for yourself or for me. You'll be doing it for Jeb and the whole *Welcome the Wind* team."

Jeb started calling for Kellie, so she had to finish quickly. "Thanks. I hear you, Jemma. Feel better! I gotta go!"

She took another deep breath as she ended the call and slid her phone into her pocket.

"Well?" Jeb said when he drew near. "What did you decide? Is it a yes or a no?"

Kellie took a deep, deep breath. She thought about arguments between brothers and sisters. She thought about how much depended on the answer she gave the worried young director.

"It's a yes," she said quietly. "I may not turn out to be any good at acting, but I promise you I'll do the very best I can."

Chapter 11

After that everything happened fast.

First, Kellie was rushed off to the costume trailer and dressed in the faded overalls and red shirt that Martha wore throughout the movie. Then it was to the makeup trailer where they toned down her natural tan, shaped her face with carefully applied foundation and shaders, then parted her hair and arranged it in two untidy braids. When Kellie looked at herself in the mirror, she thought the makeup and new hairstyle had taken two or three years off her real age.

Next, she was introduced for the first time to Jemma's co-star, Josh Collier. "Josh has had a couple of days off from filming," Harry explained when he took Kellie to meet him at the entrance to the red barn. "He got back on set late last night. Maybe you've seen him on TV?"

Kellie gulped and stared — she couldn't help it. Josh Collier played Ethan, a doctor's son in *Mayberry General*, her favorite daytime soap. He was sixteen years old and the hottest thing on the show — six feet two of hunky adorableness with deep brown eyes, dark hair, and a smoldering voice.

"Hey," Josh said, staring back at Kellie. "Wow, Harry told me you were Jemma's double but I didn't think the resemblance would be this close. This is crazy!"

"Hey," Kellie replied. She said nothing else, partly because there wasn't time, but mostly because she was so in awe of screen-hunk Josh that she couldn't think of anything to say.

"Come on, let's go," Harry urged as he led the way inside the barn. Jeb was already inside, giving instructions to his camera and lighting crews.

Kellie picked her way through dozens of cables that snaked across the floor then sidled into the last stall in the row. As her eyes adapted first to the dim light of the interior and then to the dazzle of the spotlights, she realized the stall wasn't empty as she'd expected.

"Dylan!" she gasped when she saw his cute

head peering over the stall door. He nickered back at her, and right away she felt some of her nervous tension dissolve. "Is he in the scene too?" she asked Jeb.

The director nodded. "The fight with your brother is about Sacramento, so having the horse in the scene makes sense. It goes like this — we get your back view running toward Sacramento's stall. Your brother, Matt, runs after you. His line is, 'Where are you going? They're all in the truck waiting for you.' You reach the stall door. He grabs your arm and pulls you back. You break free and push him away. He falls against this partition, here. Okay so far?"

"Yeah," Kellie replied. Run toward Dylan, get grabbed by Josh, fight him, and shove him away. That didn't sound so hard.

"Then your line is, 'I'm not coming with you!' Pretty agitated, shouting at the top of your voice, squeezing out a few tears if that's possible. 'You hear me, Matt — I'm staying here with Sacramento!'"

"I'm not coming with you!" Kellie mouthed the words, trying to get them to stick in her head. "You hear me, Matt — I'm staying here with Sacramento!" Phew, she could remember them.

She was less confident about manufacturing the tears, though.

Jeb nodded again. "At which point big brother Matt gives up on you. His line is, 'Fine! Find your own way to California — what's it to me?' He runs back the way he came. The camera closes in on you as you turn toward Sacramento and put your arms around his neck. End of scene."

∞ ◦ ∞

"Action!"

Kellie kept two things in mind as the cameras began to roll. *Number one — whip up some genuine anger by remembering how mad you were when the boys spooked Dylan on the Jeep trail and you lost your cool with Tom. Number two — imagine how brokenhearted you would've been if Dylan had been permanently lamed and had never been able to work again.*

She ran down the barn toward Dylan, hearing Josh's footsteps following her. *Don't trip, and don't mess this up*, she thought.

"Where are you going?" Josh yelled. "They're all in the truck waiting for you."

She reached the stall door, felt Josh grab her

left arm and jerk her back. The cameras were on them, the lights so strong that she felt their warmth on her skin as she twisted around and wrenched her arm free, shoving Josh hard against the partition.

Oops — too hard. He went down heavily onto the straw-strewn floor.

"I'm not coming with you!" Kellie gasped, pulling back and catching hold of the door to keep her balance. Winded, Josh groaned and rolled on to his side.

Is that real or is he acting? she wondered. She, too, was out of breath. *Think of poor Dylan, leg injured, limping along in pain.* Her heart pounded and when she spoke, there was a choking sound in her throat and hot tears came into her eyes. "You hear me, Matt — I'm staying here with Sacramento!"

"Fine!" Josh yelled as he scrambled to his feet.

Kellie choked back a sob. She took a step to follow him then turned and looked at Dylan, whose soulful eyes were fixed on her face — *Don't leave me!*

"Find your own way to California — what's it to me!" Josh delivered his line before running from the barn.

Don't worry, I'm staying right here! Kellie promised silently as she advanced toward Dylan and put her arms around his neck.

∽ ◦ ∾

"And you told me you couldn't act!" Jeb was a happy man. Kellie had gotten the scene in one take, and now he could move right to an exterior scene where the family of migrant workers — Mom, Dad, two kid brothers, and Matt — drove off without Martha.

"I honestly didn't think I could," she said.

"You were amazing — we got tears and everything."

"Thanks." Privately she was grateful to Dylan for giving her that final, pleading, don't-leave-me stare. Without him, she would never have gotten the emotion so perfect.

"No — thank you!" Jeb smiled broadly as he put his arm around Kellie's shoulder. "You put us back on track."

"Yeah, but she almost cracked my ribs," Josh joked, rubbing his sore side. "She was deadly serious when she shoved me against that partition!"

"Sorry." Kellie blushed.

"I guess I'll have to cowboy up." He put on a tough-guy look, but then his face relaxed into a grin. "Somebody should sign this girl up for a major movie. Or sign them both — Jemma and Kellie. They could play twins!"

Heart fluttering, and at a loss for words, Kellie was relieved to hear Lizzie calling her from inside the barn. "Gotta go," she told Jeb and Josh.

She found Lizzie strapping Dylan's bridle in place and checking his cinch. "So you definitely saved the day, but don't let the success go to your head," Lizzie warned in her down-to-earth way. She shortened Dylan's cinch strap by an extra hole.

"Who are you talking to? Me or Dylan?" Kellie wanted to know.

"Both." Lizzie grinned. "You did a great job standing in for Jemma, but now it's back to the nitty-gritty work." There was a tricky play-dead stunt to rehearse and very little time to do it. As usual, the Stardust trainer was set on perfection.

∽ ◦ ℃

"I see you're back working with smelly old cows," Josh commented as Kellie rode Dylan into the holding pen after supper that evening.

She shrugged. "I'm a stunt rider. It's what we do," she mumbled, still scarcely able to get her tongue around words with more than one syllable when the star actor was around. But just wait until she told Hayley and the other girls back at Stardust that she'd actually acted opposite teen-idol Josh Collier — then she'd definitely have plenty to say!

Dylan and Kellie had worked hard with Lizzie for most of the day. They had rehearsed the cattle stampede separately from the second half of the stunt, where Dylan had to jump the fence in front of a slowly moving vintage truck.

This was the trickiest part, Kellie had discovered. At first, poor Dylan had jumped and instinctively shied away from the vehicle, wanting to set off at a gallop in the opposite direction. She'd had to steer him toward the truck then bail at exactly the right moment, leaving him to roll and lie in the dirt as the truck continued to crawl toward him. Now, after rehearsing, they had to pull the two parts of the stunt together for the cameras.

"It'll be tricky, but you and Dylan can pull it off," Lizzie assured her, holding open the gate to the crowded holding pen.

Kellie nodded. She'd decided to let Dylan rest after his hot, hard day's work by leaving him in the meadow while she went for supper. By the time she came back for him, the sun had sunk behind the mountains, and the first bright stars had begun to appear in the sky.

"Remember, it'll feel different doing the stunt in the dark," Lizzie warned her. "For starters, Jeb has set up lights to mimic moonlight — high over there on the roof of the barn, and over there by the dirt track. Don't let Dylan get distracted. Also, there will be cameras everywhere."

"Okay." Kellie decided to walk her horse around each set of lights and each camera. Technicians worked busily alongside production assistants while a driver left a vintage truck idling nearby. "You have to focus," she told Dylan. "Ignore everything that's going on around us — just concentrate on what we have to do."

Chill as ever, Dylan walked calmly among the cattle, paying attention to every detail of his surroundings. When a cameraman came by to pass on the message that Jeb was being held up by an unexpected phone call, Kellie decided to ride Dylan out of the pen for a short warm up before filming.

"Good idea," Lizzie agreed. "We need Dylan to be fresh and alert when Jeb calls for action."

So Kellie walked him back to his meadow, enjoying the slice of moon she glimpsed between the aspens. "We'll soon be ready to roll," she promised Dylan, whose hooves swished through the cool grass. "Meanwhile, we can relax."

∽ ◦ ⌒

"Sorry, sorry, sorry!" Jeb was full of apologies when he finally showed up.

The phone call must have been important because the director was a full forty-five minutes late and the mood on set had grown edgy. An assistant had needed to fill the tank of the vintage truck with extra gas, two lights had blown because of the wait, and the cows had grown unsettled by the howls of coyotes higher up the mountain.

"Are we ready to go?" Jeb checked. "You've all had a long day, so we'll get through this scene as fast as we can. If we're lucky, one take should do it."

No pressure, Kellie thought. The cattle were still nervous and restless. Even Dylan seemed less relaxed than before. "Wish us luck," she said to Lizzie.

"You won't need it," Lizzie assured her. "Just wait for Jeb to call action. Then go for it."

On the far side of the fence, Jeb was giving directions to the actor playing the ranch hand who drove the truck. "You reach the fourth fence post, lean out of the cab, and without saying a word you fire." Jeb turned to Kellie. "You wait for him to fire the shot. Then you start your stunt sequence."

"Okay!" she yelled, taking a deep breath. Dylan lifted his head, and he grew more alert as the actor got behind the wheel and backed the truck out of the shot.

"Ready!" Kellie whispered.

But still they had to wait a while longer under the moon and stars, among the restless cattle. Coyotes called again — a high, nerve-tingling howl.

"Action!" Jeb cried at last.

The truck driver set off along the track, headlights swinging toward the holding pen, catching Kellie and Dylan in their beam. Then, when he reached the fourth fence post, he leaned out of the cab and fired.

Dylan reared so suddenly that Kellie's head jerked backward and her straw hat fell off. The cattle scattered. Already spooked by the coyotes, they bunched together against the fence rails, buffeting each other in their desire to get away.

Kellie felt Dylan's hindquarters slide to the right and felt herself simultaneously being flung to the left. She quickly righted herself in the saddle in time to let Dylan rear again.

By now the thirty or so cattle had bunched against the rails, banging against the fence and knocking into each other. Landing a second time, Dylan barely missed coming down on the broad back of one of the cows. It barged into two or three others. They pressed up against the fence until their combined weight suddenly broke the top rail.

Shocked, Kellie heard the sharp crack and the sound of splintering wood. There was a gap in the fence, and cattle were stampeding through.

Dylan reared and landed. He saw the cows caught in the headlights of the slowly advancing truck. He hadn't expected this. He turned his head toward Kellie, who squeezed her legs against his sides and urged him on. They would try to carry on with the stunt, forward into the space left by the stampeding cattle, ready to leap the remains of the fence into a dazzle of yellow lights and the throaty rumble of the truck's engine.

They soared through the air. The driver kept the truck coming. As Dylan landed, a cow lurched into him, knocking him off balance and shoving him out of the path of the oncoming truck. Kellie grabbed the saddle horn to stay on board. She neck-reined Dylan and tried to steer him back so they could complete the stunt. But now other cows barged through the broken fence and came between them and the truck.

"Cut!" Jeb called. The cameras stopped and the lights dimmed. It was no good — the stunt had ended in chaos.

∽ ◎ ℃

"It wasn't your fault," Lizzie said firmly to Kellie in the relative calm of Dylan's compound.

In the background, Kellie could hear men hammering, rapidly repairing the fence. They'd lost at least thirty cows, so Harry had sent a few men off in pursuit of the missing cattle while he and Jeb had rolled up their sleeves to keep the rest inside the pen.

"I feel bad." Kellie sighed and put an arm around Dylan's neck.

"It was definitely not something anyone could have predicted." Lizzie gave Dylan a thorough examination, paying particular attention to his legs and feet. "You did everything you could to make it work."

Kellie hung her head. "We really wanted to get it right."

"At least no one got hurt." Satisfied that the horse was sound, Lizzie stepped back.

"Those poor cows," Kellie said. She pictured them up on the mountain, where packs of stealthy and hungry coyotes roamed.

"Don't worry, the guys will find them and bring them back," Lizzie assured her. "We have to be ready to repeat the play-dead stunt — that's if Jeb wants us to do it again tonight, and I think he will."

"But it's nine-thirty. Everyone's tired." *Including me and Dylan*, Kellie thought, digging the heel of her boot into the ground.

Taking a look at her downcast face, which was pale in the moonlight, Lizzie put an arm around her shoulder and gave her a quick squeeze. "Chin up," she murmured. "If anyone can pull this off tonight, it's you two."

Kellie glanced up. "Really?"

"Yes, really. And you want to know why? It's because of all the riders at Stardust, you have the most guts and determination."

"No way," Kellie protested. She thought of Alisa and the elegant, flawless way she performed her stunts, then of Kami, whose sweet face and shy ways disguised the fact that she'd pretty much been born in the saddle, and then of Becca, who'd been at Stardust for the longest time. There was also Hayley, definitely the joker of the pack, but she had inherited her riding talent from her mom and obviously had a long, successful career ahead of her.

Lizzie looked her in the eye. "I mean it, Kellie. You're not loud and you're not out there in everyone's faces — that's not your personality. But every time I watch you ride and I see your natural skill and commitment, I can honestly say with all my heart that I'm proud that you're on my team."

"Thanks," Kellie mumbled.

"But don't let it go to your head." Her trainer

grinned, breaking the serious mood. "Just tuck it away in the back of your mind and remember it whenever you have doubts about your ability."

"Okay, I will."

"And now it's time to look after your horse. Give him a drink of water and some attention while we wait to see what happens next."

Chapter 12

By ten o'clock the fence was fixed. The remaining cattle were milling around inside the pen, and the truck and its driver were back in their starting position. Jeb was running through details with his technical crews, looking at his watch and glancing up at the sky to check weather conditions.

"Will he go again?" Harry asked, standing beside Kellie and Lizzie and pointing out to them that the makeup and costume crews were standing by.

"Five dollars says he will," Lizzie said.

"I think you're right," Harry told her. "Jeb is under incredible pressure to shoot this movie on time and within budget."

Kellie waited nervously.

"Okay, everyone, get into position," Jeb called eventually.

Kellie took a deep breath and quickly went to fetch Dylan from his field. "You heard what the man said," she told him, hopping onto his back and riding him toward the pen.

"Good luck," Lizzie told her as she opened the gate. "Stay focused. And now might be the time to remember what I said earlier."

Kellie nodded, walked her horse through the gate, and took up her position among the cattle. *So far, so good.*

"Good boy," she breathed, hoping that the coyotes wouldn't spook the cattle a second time. That was the one thing that was beyond everyone's control.

If anyone can pull this off tonight, it's you two. Lizzie's recent compliment came through loud and clear as Kellie and Dylan waited the last few, tense minutes before the director called action.

"Ready? We can do this," she told Dylan. His calmness had settled her nerves, so now they both had exactly the right level of adrenaline flowing through their veins.

Of all the riders at Stardust, you have the most guts and determination.

"We can do it!" Kellie said again, her hands soft on the reins.

The lights were on; the cameras were ready to roll.

"Action!" Jeb called.

The truck set off, and Kellie held Dylan steady among the restless, tightly packed cattle. The truck came closer until it was parallel to the fourth fence post. The driver leaned out of the window and took aim. A coyote called across the valley — a long, lonely wail. The gun went off. Double drama.

The cows jostled and trampled the ground. Almost without Kellie having to ask him, Dylan reared high above the backs of the cattle. He flung back his head and whipped his mane from his face. He landed and then reared again, ears flattened, nostrils flared.

Kellie tried not to grin. Dylan was playing it big for the camera, determined not to let anyone steal his thunder a second time.

Up and down he went, rocking forward, scattering the cattle as he kicked out with his back feet.

This time the cows divided right down the middle, some to the left and some to the right, leaving a clear way through for Kellie and Dylan. Kellie pointed him through the gap. *Go, Dylan!*

Putting in a final, spectacular buck, her brilliant horse crow-hopped across the space. At the very last instant, he twisted to face the fence, rested on his haunches, and then sprang almost vertically into the air.

For a split second Kellie feared that he'd left it too late, that they would have no forward momentum and were going to crash straight down onto the rail. But then, with a display of superb equine athleticism and strength, Dylan cleared the fence.

Safe on the dirt track, Kellie saw the old truck bearing down on them in a blaze of headlights. Enjoying the moment, she gave a sharp kick with her left heel. Again Dylan went for the big display, deciding to turn toward the light and rear up before he went down. Kellie felt him land and dip to the right — the signal for her to scramble clear as he rolled. Horse and rider parted company. She was safely out of the saddle, hunched on the ground out of shot as Dylan lay motionless and the truck kept on coming.

"Cut!" Jeb cried. "Excellent, everyone. Really good job, Kellie!"

∽ ◦ ൏

By the time filming was finished for the night and the crews had packed away their equipment, it was eleven o'clock.

Jeb helped clear up, then stood with his arms folded and a smile on his face. "Time to get some sleep," he said. "Jemma will be back on set tomorrow and we need an early start."

"But what about the runaway cows — are they back yet?" Kellie asked Lizzie after they'd stowed Dylan's saddle in the trailer cab and gone back to check that he was okay for the night.

Lizzie shook her head. "No. Apparently it's hopeless trying to search in the dark. We need to wait until morning."

"But . . ." Kellie's imagination worked overtime. She pictured frightened cattle roaming the hillside and coyotes creeping up on them.

"No buts," Lizzie said briskly. "I agree that we need to get those cattle back, but the best thing we can do is to call around for help and set out as early as we can tomorrow morning."

"What kind of help?" Kellie wanted to ask, but Lizzie had ended the discussion, said goodnight, and walked off.

"We don't know anyone in Molly Gulch," she reminded Dylan, who'd strolled over to see her. "And I can't see Jeb giving the film crew any more time off to round up cows."

Head to one side, he seemed to be paying attention.

"But hey," Kellie went on. "What am I thinking? We do know people in Jackson Hole. Well, Hayley and her mom, anyway."

Dylan tilted his head to the other side then back again.

"I'm going to make a call." She found her contacts on her phone and selected Hayley's number. "Hey, sorry to call so late," she said

"Kellie? Why aren't you in bed?" Hayley yawned. "Don't you know what time it is?"

"Yes, but this is really important," Kellie insisted. "I need your help . . ."

∽ ◦ ℅

"I always knew Dylan was amazing," Kellie told Hayley as they rode through the aspens the next morning. "But last night, he was unbelievable!"

At sunrise, the two girls had met up at the entrance to Molly Gulch. Hayley's mom, Gina Forest, had made some late-night emergency calls to her friends in Jackson Hole looking for help.

"We need horses and riders to help bring in thirty head of cattle from the foothills," she'd told Urma Winchester from Triple Star, a guest ranch located just outside the town. "Do you know anyone who could help?"

"I sure do," Urma had replied. "There's my husband Henry and me — you can definitely count us in — plus our neighbors, the Wyatt boys from the N Bar Ranch. Yep, I can get you volunteers and horses, no problem."

And here they were at the break of dawn — a group of expert riders on their well-trained Quarter Horses. Everyone was eager to bring in the runaway cows.

"'A-maz-ing!'" Hayley listened to Kellie praise her horse and echoed her words. "'Unbelievable!'"

"What's wrong with that?" Kellie blushed.

"You wouldn't say you were a teeny bit prejudiced?" Hayley teased as Lizzie organized the volunteers.

"Nope." Kellie grinned back. "I'm just giving you my professional opinion!"

"We'll split into pairs," Lizzie decided once everyone had unloaded their horses from the trailers and saddled up. "That way we can cover more territory."

So the young Wyatt brothers, Justin and Cody, set off on matching Appaloosas deep into the steep-sided valley, looking for tracks and for any other sign left by the cows. Lizzie and Gina took a higher route toward a known clearing where cattle might gather, while Henry and Urma Winchester decided to follow the Jeep road ending at the rocky outcrop and good vantage point called Medicine Ridge.

This left Kellie and Hayley to ride around the edge of Dylan's meadow, through the aspens into the pine forest beyond.

"So what exactly happened last night?" Hayley asked.

"It was crazy," Kellie explained, more than happy to relive the whole experience. "We'd rehearsed everything until it was perfect, of course — you know how Lizzie is. Well, anyway, there was a delay before Jeb finally arrived on set, which meant nothing went as planned because by that time the cattle knew there were coyotes up in the hills. They didn't like that one little bit."

"What about Dylan? Was he stressed too?"

"No, he just wanted to get to work." Kellie let her sure-footed horse pick his way across a narrow creek that ran over rocks and between the trees. She waited at the far side for Hayley and her horse, Tucker, to follow. Tucker, a dappled gray Quarter Horse who belonged to the Triple Star string, seemed edgy.

"It's because he's off-trail in territory he's not familiar with," Hayley told Kellie. "Good little guy. You can do it," she murmured as he stumbled across the creek then lurched up the steep bank. He wasn't as bold as Cool Kid back at Stardust, so she gave him plenty of encouragement. "So what did Dylan do after the cattle broke down the fence?" she asked.

"He turns his head and takes one look at me, like he's asking, 'What do we do now?' I tell him, 'We do our job.' And he goes ahead and jumps that old fence like a pro, ready to play dead like nothing's wrong. Only, the cows have a different idea. They get in between us and the truck and throw us off course. They ruined the whole thing."

"And did Jeb make you do it over again?" Still curious, Hayley brought Tucker alongside Dylan, and they walked further into the aspens.

"He sure did," Kellie told her. "He said the stampede may not have been in the script but it looked spectacular. So he wants to put sections of it into the final cut. But yeah, we had to run the actual play-dead sequence a second time. Luckily it went well. In fact, do you want to know what Jeb said after we finished?"

"Not really, but I guess you're going to tell me, anyway."

"He told us that was the best stunt sequence he'd ever filmed! Dylan was amazing."

"Wow!" Hayley was happy for her friend. But suddenly she had other things on her mind. "Look here," she told Kellie, pointing to sets of footprints in soft, sandy ground. "What are these, deer or cows?"

"Too big for deer," Kelly decided. "So I'd say cows, and they're doubling back toward that bunch of willows by the creek we just crossed."

"Yeah, I see them." Hayley was excited. In fact, she was the first to make out several black shapes rustling through the bushes. No doubt about it, they'd found some of the missing animals. "Come on, girl," she told Kellie. "Let's get busy. It's round-up time!"

Chapter 13

"Twenty-four, twenty-five . . ." Back at Molly Gulch, Lizzie counted Hayley and Kellie's cows into the small pen by the red barn. " . . . twenty-eight, twenty-nine, thirty. That's it — we reached our target!"

In the end, the girls had driven seven cows out of the willows by the creek and pushed them back down the mountain. Naturally, the cows hadn't wanted to come — they'd gotten over their fear of the coyotes and preferred to roam and graze at will — but Dylan and Tucker had worked hard all morning. They stuck at their herd work across the creek and through the aspens until the film set came into view.

"Gina and I found twelve, the Winchesters brought in seven, which left four for the Wyatt boys to pick up in the gulch. That's a grand total of thirty," said Lizzie.

"High five!" a delighted Hayley said to her cowgirl buddy.

Kellie grinned back at her. "High five!" she agreed.

∞ ◦ ∞

"So this is the scene where Matt comes back for Martha," Jeb explained to the crew as they gathered outside the red barn.

It was Monday afternoon, and there was an upbeat atmosphere on the set of *Welcome the Wind* after the morning's successful roundup and the return of Jemma from Jackson Hole.

"I'm so glad you're feeling better," said Kellie. "It lets me off the acting hook."

"I heard you did a good job," Jemma said. "In fact, I was worried you might be too good."

"Not a chance!" Kellie laughed modestly, then introduced Jemma to Hayley.

"You remember me?" Hayley asked.

"Of course! You rode the Paint horse in the auditions at Stardust. You made a really big impression."

"Would that be a good or a bad thing?"

"You're kidding, right? You were my favorite!

No offense, Kellie. It's just that I loved that bold little Paint."

"I've been visiting family in Jackson Hole," Hayley said as the three girls went to the catering tent for a late breakfast of coffee and a bacon sandwich. "I came to help round up the runaway cows, then I decided to camp out here with Kellie tonight so we can get an early start tomorrow. It's a twelve-hour drive —" She stopped suddenly when Jemma sat them down at the same table as Josh. "Whoa, swoon-fest!" she muttered behind her hand.

"I know," Kellie whispered back. "He's even hotter in person than he is on TV."

Hayley stared at Josh. "Give me a pen," she squealed at Kellie. "Quick, I have to have his autograph!"

But she wasn't fast enough, because Josh disappeared into the makeup trailer to get ready for his scene with Jemma.

"Major, major swoon alert!" Hayley said with a sigh.

Kellie laughed in agreement. Meeting actors like Josh Collier was definitely one of the perks to the stunt-riding business. Now they were both looking forward to seeing him in action.

"Matt comes back for Martha because he's heard about her accident with Sacramento." Jeb greeted his two main actors and then gave them the background to the scene they were about to shoot. "He's been told the horse is dead. He knows that his sister will be absolutely heartbroken."

"Is that true?" Hayley whispered frantically at Kellie as they watched from a distance. "Does Sacramento die?"

Kellie shrugged. "Nobody's told me what happens after the truck crashes into him."

"But you and Dylan don't have any more scenes?"

"No. So, yeah, I guess poor Sacramento does die in the accident."

"This scene between Matt and Martha is gonna make me cry," Hayley predicted.

"Why? It's only a story," Kellie pointed out, glancing over her shoulder. There was a perfectly healthy Dylan contentedly grazing in his compound. Then she quoted from the end film credits that would roll up the screen. "'The producers wish to state that no equine was harmed in the making of this movie.'"

"But Josh is so talented, and I love him so

much. I mean it, Kellie. He's gonna make me cry my eyes out!"

∽ ◦ ℃

"What's wrong with Hayley — why is she mooning around like a lovesick calf?" Lizzie asked Kellie as she drove the trailer out of Molly Gulch early on Tuesday morning.

There was a pink glow in the eastern sky, but the sun had yet to rise and the air was gray and chilly. Except for the Stardust trailer bumping and swaying along the rutted road with Dylan in the back, there was no sign of life on set.

"She finally got Josh Collier's autograph," Kellie explained, sitting between Lizzie and Hayley. Hayley took out a tissue and blew her nose loudly.

Last night, after the end of filming, Hayley had cornered her movie idol. He had signed his name in black felt-tip pen on the back of her T-shirt and even posed for a photo with his arm around her shoulder. Hayley had quickly posted it on Facebook.

"And she's unhappy about that?" said Lizzie with a puzzled frown.

"No, ignore the sniffles. She's actually really happy!" Kellie explained the reasons for Hayley's emotional mood. "First thing — she witnessed the big reunion scene between Matt and Martha. Sacramento's dead and Martha's alone in the world, remember."

Enthusiastically Hayley joined in with the explanation. "Enter big brother Matt on a vintage motorbike. He rides along Medicine Ridge, looking down on to Molly Gulch. He cuts across the country, churning up clouds of dust. He finds Martha walking alone along a dirt road to nowhere. He overtakes her and then throws the bike to the ground. He takes a step toward his kid sister and holds out his hand in a gesture of brotherly love."

"Very intense," Lizzie murmured, trying not to smile at Hayley's vivid description.

"Reason number two for Hayley to be crying," Kellie went on. "Josh's autograph and the picture. Enough said. Reason three — Josh and Jemma gave us their phone numbers. They definitely, definitely want to visit Stardust and chill for a few days after they've finished making *Welcome the Wind*."

"And reason number four," Hayley said, "is

just everything that's happened in the last few days. Visiting my family, rounding up cattle, meeting my screen idol, watching the filming, driving back to Stardust to work with Cool Kid again, and hopefully get a job — everything!"

"How about you?" Lizzie asked Kellie as they reached the highway and headed south. "Are you pleased with the way the job went?"

Kellie slid down in her seat and put her feet up on the dashboard. "Yeah, I totally am," she said, settling down to think about her own highlights on the long journey home.

∽ ◦ ∾

"So?" Tom asked his sister as they scooped poop in the corral early the next morning.

"So?" Kellie echoed. Knowing that it would wind Tom up, she decided to make him wait before she shared the details about her time in Wyoming.

"So did you go ahead with your acting debut?"

"I did, yeah."

"How was it?"

"Actually good, thanks."

"And how did Dylan do in his stunt scenes?"

"He did good."

"And?"

"And . . . what?"

"His injured leg held up okay?"

"Yeah, fine." Sleeves rolled up, she scooped and threw muck into the trailer, whistling as she worked.

"How did he do working with cows?"

"Really good."

Tom stopped work and leaned on his rake. "What's up, Kellie?" he said with a frown. "Are you still mad at me?"

"Maybe." She went around the corral scooping and whistling. But it was no good, she couldn't keep up this don't-bother-me-I'm-busy act any longer. "No, I'm not mad at you!" she declared with a wide grin. "I'm just enjoying pushing your buttons."

"So we're cool?" He grinned back.

She nodded. "If you really want to know — and I know you do — Dylan proved he was the best cow horse ever. Plus, he was amazing in the play-dead sequence. What more can I say?"

"Nothing. That's all good. Everyone's happy." Tom jumped up into the tractor to drive the trailer out to the muckheap. "By the way, Kami, Ross, and Becca got back yesterday."

"I know. They were already in bed when we arrived."

"They loved Connecticut," he told her. "Kami says she learned a whole lot about natural horsemanship from the head wrangler there, and Jack wants to develop the techniques here at Stardust. That'll be very cool."

"So how are things with Kami?" Kellie asked, walking alongside the tractor as Tom set off out of the corral.

"Good, thanks."

"And?"

"And . . . ?" he stonewalled. Two could play at that game.

"Ha, very good — touché!" Laughing, she let him drive off. She ran to the dorm to take a quick shower before going to the ranch house for breakfast, where she found Becca, Alisa, and Kami swooning over Hayley's signed T-shirt.

"I'm going to pin it to my bedroom wall above the picture of me and Josh," Hayley vowed. "I'm going to keep it forever."

Kellie was about to join them, but she held back. They were happy. She was happy.

Everything was good. Tom joined her at the door. "What can I get you for breakfast — the usual three pieces of bacon with two eggs over-easy?"

She shook her head. "Later," she told him.

First she wanted to see Dylan. She went out to the meadow and sat on the fence, watching him raise his head from grazing and then make his usual beeline toward her.

"Hey," she told him, reaching out and gently patting his neck.

He nudged her with his nose, then gave her a sudden, hard shove.

"Whoa!" She started to tip back and had to grab the fence rail with both hands to save herself from falling to the ground. "Good thing I have lightning-quick reactions!"

Dylan shoved again, and this time Kellie somersaulted backward off the fence. "What's going on, boy? What's up?"

He tossed his head and trotted down the fence line until he reached the gate.

She followed him. He pushed at the latch with his nose.

"I get it. You want us to go for a ride!" Kellie realized. She looked across the meadow to the stand of pine trees growing at the foot of

Clearwater Peak — the mountain she knew and loved — and above its white summit, she saw the pale shape of last night's waxing moon in the pure blue sky.

"Okay, let's do it," she told Dylan. They would spend the morning in the mountains together. The sun would shine and there would be no one around. They would be perfectly free.

About the Author

Sable Hamilton is the pen name for Jenny Oldfield, author of a wide range of books for children and young adults — including the internationally successful mini series Beautiful Dead and Dark Angel. With Stardust Stables, she has returned to one of her favorite subjects — the glamour, the thrills, and the trials of working with horses!

Glossary

camaraderie (kah-muh-RAH-duh-ree) — good feelings of friendship and feeling like you are all working on the same team

charade (shuh-REYD) — a very obvious lie or deception

dejection (di-JEK-shuhn) — depression or not feeling in a good mood

dressing (DRES-ing) — a covering or bandage for a wound

infection (in-FEKT-shuhn) — an illness or disease caused by bacteria or a virus

lame (LAYM) — having trouble walking because of sickness or injury

partition (pahr-TISH-uhn) — a panel that divides a room or area

recuperate (ri-KOO-puh-rate) — to heal and get better after an injury or illness

retaliate (ri-TAL-ee-ate) — to react to an injury or insult with similar behavior

rival (RYE-vuhl) — one of two or more people who is trying to get what only one person can have

swoon (SWOON) — to faint or become weak or dizzy because of great emotion

More about Horses

bridle (BRYE-duhl) — a harness that goes on a horse's head and allows a person to control and guide the horse

canter (KAN-tur) — a medium-fast speed, faster than a trot but slower than a gallop

corral (kuh-RAL) — a fenced-in area that holds livestock, such as horses or cows

halter (HAWL-tur) — a strap that fits behind the ears and over the nose, used to lead or tie an animal like a horse

lope (LOHP) — a Western term for canter, but may be a more easy-going and relaxed speed than a canter

palomino (pal-uh-MEE-noh) — a horse with a golden coat and white mane and tail

Paint (PEYNT) — a breed of horse that has a spotted coat

tack (TAK) — all of the things you need to ride a horse, like a saddle and bridle

trot (TRAHT) — a speed that's in between walking and running, slower than a canter or gallop

Discussion Questions

1. The girls didn't think that the boys' ambush was a funny prank. Have people ever played a prank on you that they thought was funny, but you didn't? Talk about your experience.

2. Discuss reasons why Kellie would be nervous about standing in for Jemma. What do you think made her finally agree to acting in the scene?

3. Kellie really likes being out in nature because she feels free. Do you like being outside or going camping? Why or why not?

Writing Prompts

1. The riders at Stardust Stables are only there for the summer. What do you during the summer? Write about one summer that you really enjoyed.

2. It takes lots of people to make a movie: actors, directors, stunt people, makeup artists, hairstylists, costume-makers, special effects people, etc. If you could choose any job in a movie, what would you do? Why?

3. Imagine your dream horse. Write a story about an adventure that you have with your horse.

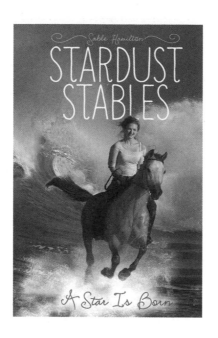

A Star Is Born

Kami is super excited about joining Stardust Stables and quickly falls in love with her gorgeous horse, Magic. When the chance arises to try out for the role of stunt double to starlet Coreen Kessler, her dreams are close to coming true! Kami knows she has a good shot at getting the part — but so does seasoned stunt rider Becca, and there's no way Becca's going to step aside and let Kami take the role . . .